W9-CCO-911

Scotty and the Gypsy Bandit

Scotty
and the Gypsy Bandit

DAVID WINKLER

Farrar Straus Giroux

New York

Library of Congress Cataloging-in-Publication Data
Winkler, David, date.
    Scotty and the Gypsy Bandit / David Winkler.
        p.   cm.
    Summary: Twelve-year-old Scotty watches the strange behavior
of his friend and neighbor McStew turn their street into a carnival
and fears that it is changing his life in drastic ways.
    ISBN 0-374-36420-6
    [1. Neighbors—Fiction.   2. Friendship—Fiction.   I. Title.
PZ7.W72927Sc   2000
[Fic]—dc21   99-33340

To Morgan

Princess of Light

Contents

Scotty and the Gypsy Bandit

Castle in the Sky

"See where those branches cross? That's where the floor will go." My father pointed to a spot a million miles off the ground.

"Why so high up?" I asked.

"That's where I built a tree house when *I* was in fifth grade. Of course, Audrey's grown since then, but"— Dad patted the oak's trunk like it was an old friend— "that means you and I can build an even bigger one. We can rent part of it out if we like. What do you say?"

"I don't think so," was what I said.

"Oh, come on, Scotty, it'll be fun."

"I want to play ball."

"Great idea! We can toss a few around while we plan our tree house."

What I'd meant was, I wanted to go play ball with my friends, but Dad didn't get it. "Won't this be great?

Father and son working side by side." He squinted up. "Castle in the Sky."

It was spring, 1959, and Audrey was bright with buds.

I hurried into the house and nearly tripped over Toby, my mother's gray cat, who was always in the way. The week before, he'd carried off two of my baseball cards, one a Mickey Mantle.

"What's with Dad?" I said, reaching into the refrigerator for the milk.

"Scotty, use a glass!" Mom shouted from the dining room.

I wiped my mouth with my sleeve just as she came charging around the corner.

"All of a sudden he wants to be buddy-buddy," I told her.

She filled my hands with silverware and led me back to the dining room. "You're his son," she said. "He wants to spend time with you."

"That's a laugh."

Mom spun around in a way that made me think she might crack a plate over my head. But all she did was stare her stare.

"Go tell him dinner's ready," she said.

Dad was still standing under the tree, gazing into its branches and measuring angles with his fingers. All through dinner he talked about the tree house and how it would have walls and a roof and a pantry.

"A *pantry*?" I echoed.

"Sure, why not? Castle in the Sky." He winked at Mom, and I looked at her for a sign that she knew he'd gone completely nuts, but all she did was reach for the spinach. "Let's see," he said. "Tomorrow's Saturday—"

"Friday," I corrected him. "Tomorrow's Friday."

"Friday. Right. So Saturday's the next day. We'll start early and get the floor in by, say, noon. I'll order the materials. But first—first I'd better go draw up some plans." He threw down his napkin and sped away from the table, muttering to himself on his way up the stairs.

"Mom."

"It won't kill you to build a tree house with your father," she said. "Try being cooperative. This once."

They were both nuts.

I excused myself and went to find McStew, our next-door neighbor. He was nuts, too, but in a way I could handle. He was digging a hole in his back yard.

"I buried treasure out here last fall," McStew said, "but I can't remember where."

"What kind of treasure?" I asked.

"You'd be surprised." There were holes all over the place. "Here, you can use Reese's shovel while he takes a break. But we need to hurry." Reese was McStew's make-believe friend. I knew there was no treasure, but I started digging anyway.

"My dad's flipped his noodle," I said. "He wants to build a tree house."

"When can we start?"

"You don't get it." I felt my shovel strike something hard. "As long as I've known him he's never wanted to do anything, not even go to a ball game. His job keeps him too busy. Now all of a sudden—"

"A tree house! Why didn't *you* think of that?" Mc-

Stew spoke to the invisible person behind him. "That's where we'll hide the treasure. But first we've got to find it."

"There's something down here," I said.

"Hey, that's it!" McStew dropped his shovel and pawed at the ground like a dog. "Oh, crap. It's only my mom's sewing machine."

"Her what?"

"Cover it back up. Hurry!"

"Hey, Scotty!" Dad's head poked out of his bedroom window. "What do you say we put in a library? We can read to each other!"

"I can't take this," I whispered, and laid down the shovel. I started walking toward the street.

"Hey, Durango, where you going?" McStew called after me.

"Montana. Australia. Somewhere far away."

"Ya hear that, Reese? Montana! Saddle up!"

The next morning, as I was about to leave for school, Dad was already out back with a ladder, a measuring tape, and a tool chest which was rusted shut because he never used it.

"You mean he's not going to work?" I asked.

"Not today," Mom answered.

"But he *always* goes to work." I spied out the window at my busy dad. "I hate building stuff. Can't you talk to him?"

"Maybe you should be the one to do that."

For the first time in my life I was sorry for the school day to end. Even Mrs. Mackley's tired old voice was music to my ears as she droned on about math and

English and other useless stuff. I couldn't picture my-self a hundred feet off the ground hammering and saw-ing away at something I didn't care about in the first place. And it wasn't that I was scared of heights. I'd climbed the oak hundreds of times and liked playing in her branches. I knew where all the bent and rusty nails were, left over from when Dad was a kid. The problem was Dad himself. As far back as third grade I gave up asking him to play ball, go camping or fishing, or any-thing else fun, because his job at the oil company ate up all his time. It was always, "Not now, Scotty. Not today. Can't you see I'm busy?" Now here he was staying home from work to build a tree house.

I dragged my feet all the way home and when I got there the nightmare was waiting. In the back yard, set up on concrete blocks, was a stack of building materi-als—plywood, two-by-fours, rolls of tar paper, a bucket of nails—I don't know what all.

Mom came rushing out. "Pretend you're happy."

"Pretend I'm happy? This'll take all weekend. I have a ball game!" I objected.

"Well, think of it this way," Mom said. "You'll learn some carpentry."

"I'll learn that in junior high."

"Now, listen. He put considerable expense into order-ing"—Mom waved her hand at the pile of stuff—"that. Right now he's taking a nap. So you'd better think about what you're going to do before he wakes up." And she went inside.

I stared up at my parents' bedroom window. A nap? Him?

Just over the hedge, in the next yard, I heard sounds of digging. It crossed my mind to get McStew to help Dad build the tree house. It was more up his alley than mine, but I figured he'd be more nuisance than help. At school, kids called him "McScrew-loose," a nickname for a nickname. His real name was Mick Stewart, but everyone called him McStew, even the teachers. "Call me whatever you want," he told them, "but my real name's the Gypsy Bandit." He had nicknames for everybody. He called me Durango.

"So here's my idea," said Dad after his nap. He stood with his hands on his hips, grinning up at Audrey. I stood a short distance away. Lately he'd been doing weird stuff like tousling my hair, putting his hands on my shoulders, and once he even tried to hug me. "One of us'll stay here on the ground—me—and the other'll be up in the tree—you. We'll devise a pulley and hoist everything up. As long as we follow this"—he whipped out his plan, a crumpled piece of yellow paper with blue markings—"we'll do fine." I could feel splinters in my hands already.

"Dad. Can I say something?"

"No, no, don't thank me." Dad came over and patted me on the shoulder. "There'll be plenty of time for that later. And once we're done? You and I'll sleep up there."

"We'll what?"

"Every night if you like." He winked. "Don't worry. I'll clear it with you-know-who." Suddenly I felt like crawling into one of McStew's holes. Dad rubbed his hands together and said, "I know what you're thinking. We might as well get started while there's still daylight. I agree!"

Right then I let out a howl and dropped to my knees, holding my middle.

"Scotty—son—what's wrong?"

"It's—my stomach," I groaned.

"Oh, my God!—Marie, Marie, come quick!—Scotty, don't move, just—Marie!"

I rolled myself into a ball and tried to throw up.

"What's this?" It was Mom.

"Something's wrong with his stomach," said Dad, all panicky. "We should call an ambulance."

"We should call Hollywood," Mom said. The toe of her shoe was pointed at my eye like a six-gun.

"I'm dying," I moaned. "It must've been the school lunch."

"Come on, Frank, grab an arm. Let's get our boy up to his room," said my mother. "Saturday and Sunday in bed with a mashed vegetable diet ought to put him back on his feet in time for school on Monday."

"Don't worry, son." Dad helped hoist me up with his hand under my shoulder. "I'll read to you all weekend."

In bed, I forced myself to listen to the first two chapters of *The Swiss Family Robinson* before pretending to fall asleep. Dad put his hand on my forehead before tiptoeing out of the room. I was planning how to get out of my room *and* out of making the tree house when Mom came in. She closed the door and sat on the edge of the bed.

"You're not asleep," I heard her say, and I opened my eyes. "I guess it's time you knew," she whispered, and squeezed my hand. "It's a brain tumor."

"No, it's a stomachache," I said.

"I'm talking about your father. He was diagnosed a

while back. It's inoperable, which is why"—she bit her lower lip and took a deep breath—"which is why you might want to spend some time . . . while you can."

I just blinked at her. "What?"

"He didn't want you to know," Mom went on. "He wanted you to help him with the tree house because you *want* to, and not because—" She leaned her face close to mine. "Son, do you understand?"

Of course I didn't. Did she think that just mentioning *brain tumor* would make me leap out of bed, rush downstairs, and grab a bucket of nails? Anyway, it couldn't be true. Dad was fine.

"Go away," I said and buried my face in the pillow.

She sat there for what seemed like forever. Then I felt her touch my arm before she left the room.

Brain tumor. The words rattled around in my own brain like bent nails in a bucket.

The next morning I took my time going downstairs. It was Saturday and I was supposed to meet Corky and Ross and some other guys at Jollyman Park for a double header. Dad was at the breakfast table reading Wednesday's sports page. Mom was off buying groceries.

"Well, there's our trooper." He smiled. "How's the head?"

"Stomach." I went to the refrigerator and drank milk straight from the bottle. Toby scooted past and just for fun I tried shutting his tail in the door. "It's fine," I said.

"Great day for a tree house." Dad set aside his paper and nodded at the window while I stared at the back of his head. It looked the same as always. "I hear you have other plans."

"We can start right now if you want," I said.

Dad got up from his chair and laid his hand on my shoulder. "You go play ball, son. To tell the truth, Audrey's a little under the weather. Maybe tomorrow." And he shuffled upstairs.

I went and played ball but my heart wasn't in it. I kept striking out.

That night I said to Mom, "Is it true? Does Dad really have—what you said?"

She nodded. "It's somewhere the doctors can't get at." She was mending a rip in the trousers I'd worn that day. "Now and then he gets these awful headaches."

"I never knew."

"Of course you didn't. He didn't want you to."

"Will he—I mean, how do people get those?"

"Brain tumors? I have no idea. What I do know," said Mom, and her eyes turned a little glassy, "is we need to do everything we can here at home. To make him comfortable."

"Yeah, but can't they do something? The doctors?"

"He started chemotherapy, but—we'll see." Something in her voice worried me. "At first they were going to send him somewhere out in California, which would've been ironic because it's where I always wanted him to take me. We just never got around to it."

"We can still go," I said hopefully, and she showed me a sad smile.

My dad's family, the Hansens, had lived in the same house since the beginning of time. I think they must have moved into it the moment they stepped off the

Mayflower. Dad was somebody who worked all the time, a person who never had any fun—like ants. Mom said he got that from Granddad. "Why go moving all over creation when you've got a perfectly good home and job right here?" I remember Granddad saying to my father. "You've got roots, boy, like that tree out back."

Audrey was the name Dad gave the oak tree when he was two years old. What he really was saying was "old tree," but it sounded to everyone like "Audrey" and the name stuck.

"I suppose the lesson is, be thankful for what you've got," said my mother, "because tomorrow guarantees us nothing. The main thing you need to know, Scotty, is he regrets not spending more time with you." Just then she jabbed the sewing needle into her thumb, which blossomed with blood. "There's another lesson. Keep your mind on what you're doing."

I went and got the hydrogen peroxide. I said, "That reminds me. McStew buried his mom's sewing machine in their back yard."

"Good place for it." She poured peroxide over her thumb and we watched it fizz. "The way that woman drinks, it's a wonder she hasn't sewn her fingers together by now."

"One day she put a pot holder in the toaster and nearly burned the house down, so McStew buried the toaster."

"Maybe I should count my blessings," said Mom, staring at her thumb.

I got up on Sunday ready to spend the day up in Audrey with hammer and nails, pretending to know what I was doing. But Mom surprised me by saying Dad was still in bed.

"Is it the tumor?" I asked.

"Why don't you go read to him?" She handed me *The Swiss Family Robinson*.

I wanted to ask if there was even a tiny chance he'd get better, but I couldn't make my lips say the words. So I took the book and crept into Dad's room and sat in the stuffed chair by his bed. He lay there with his head sunk in the pillow, eyes closed, mouth open. I began to read where he'd left off. I was halfway down the page when I noticed how still he was. I leaned over and put my hand on his chest and couldn't feel a thing.

"Dad?" I said. There was no breathing. "Dad!"

I dropped the book and ran downstairs. Mom was sitting on the living-room couch reading a magazine with Toby curled up in her lap.

I said, "It's Dad, he—he's not breathing!"

Toby went sailing as Mom flew up the stairs. She bent down over my father and put her hand on his forehead. "Frank," she whispered in his ear. "Frank." And he opened his eyes. "Are you all right?"

"Fine," he said. "But—what's the matter with him?"

My face was streaked with tears and I was shaking. Both parents were staring at me. I raced down the stairs, through the house, and out across the back porch into the yard. I kicked Audrey's trunk.

"Scotty!" Mom was right behind me. I started to climb the tree but she grabbed my shoe. "Come down here."

"He did that on purpose," I said.

"He did no such a thing. It's his medication. It puts him in a deep sleep."

"Then why'd he wake up when *you* called him?"

"He responds to my voice, don't ask me why."

I wriggled loose from her and broke through the hedge to McStew's yard. He wasn't around, just his shovel and a bunch of holes. I banged on the screen door and saw Mrs. Stewart sitting at the kitchen table licking her tongue around the inside of an empty glass. Ashes dropped from her lit cigarette. She had on the black-and-blue checkered dress she never changed out of.

"Is McStew here?" I asked.

One of Mrs. Stewart's eyes was puffy and pasted shut. She said, "McWho?"

I headed for Jollyman Park and sat for a long time in one of the swings. There were no other kids.

What if Dad dies?

I leaped out of the swing and pounded my ears with my hands to keep from thinking such thoughts. I wanted him to get well and go back to work and for things to be normal, and it was okay if he never paid attention to me, I didn't care, just as long as he got better, that's all that mattered. I'd even build the tree house, or do whatever else he wanted. I ran home to tell him that. But when I got there he was asleep again and Mom was in the kitchen baking bread. She slugged the dough with her fist. Whenever Mom was upset, she baked bread. I didn't let her see me. Instead, I went off to watch TV, to forget about things.

Just when I'd changed my mind about building the

tree house, Dad changed his mind, too. He got it into his head that the old oak was in sad shape, that it suffered from some horrible disease and needed saving. Suddenly he was out there spraying stuff on it and I heard Mom say to him, "Now, Frank, you know there's not a thing wrong with that tree," but he waved her away like she was part of the problem. He trimmed the grass short around the trunk and got me to string a wire fence around it. I wondered what good a wire fence would do. When I complained to Mom, all she could say was, "Between the tumor and the medication, he gets confused. Try to be patient."

I said to Dad, "What do you think ails this old tree, anyway?" The oak stretched fat and green above the roof, practically into the clouds.

"She has a blight," Dad answered.

"What's a blight?"

"Something that kills trees."

He was busy painting the roots with some stinky-smelling chemical he'd whipped up in the basement. I thought if the tree wasn't already sick it soon would be, but I kept my mouth shut. Dad ordered me to climb up onto the branches and yank out the nails he'd hammered in years ago. The nails were rusted into the bark and you'd have to be Superman to pull them loose. All I did was rub my fingers over them and yell down that they were out. What was weird was, when I touched the nails, I saw—or thought I saw—the tree house Dad had built when he was a boy, and I pictured him crawling in and out of it. The house had blown down in a storm before I was born.

When I dropped back to the ground, Dad was sitting on the grass with his hands on his knees. He looked tuckered out. He patted the ground as a signal for me to come sit next to him.

"The thing about trees is," he said, "if you don't look after them they die. I should've remembered that. Audrey was here way before any of us Hansens showed up, long before this house was even built. My father climbed her. I ever tell you that?"

"I think you did," I said.

"Difference is, he never stuck nails in her."

I glanced over at the pile of building materials, covered with a tarp and forgotten.

"You don't go sticking nails in something you love," said my father, "and you don't turn your back on it, because that can kill it as dead as nails." He was hugging his knees up close to his chest like a little kid, and I heard him say, "Jesse."

"What?"

"I miss you."

"Who's Jesse?"

Dad jumped up so suddenly it surprised me. He grabbed the bucket with the smelly stuff and started splashing it onto the roots like it was the most important job on earth.

Of course he got worse. His hair fell out and he lost a lot of weight. Not that he was fat to begin with, but soon his belts didn't fit and, even though Mom bought him new ones, he used neckties to hold his pants up. Dad still worried about the tree. Mom sent me out with him in case he slipped. But mostly he was too busy sprinkling or spraying stuff to notice I was there. Sometimes he talked to the tree, and other times he talked to Jesse, who wasn't there. Once I saw Mom's face watching through the kitchen window, and she looked like somebody I didn't know.

Dad quit going to his job. He went to doctors instead. They gave him pills and chemo treatments and X rays and said it was okay for him to stay home as long as he wasn't in a lot of discomfort. Besides that, they told Mom, there wasn't much they could do.

"If only he'd gone in sooner," I heard Mom say from time to time, "when those headaches began. If only."

Word traveled fast. Kids at school whispered and smiled politely whenever I was around. I felt like I was in church. Mrs. Mackley said I could sit in class and not listen to her if I didn't want to, which is what I always did anyway. Everyone treated me different. Everyone except McStew.

He said, "Know what, Durango? Your dad looks like a pirate with that bandana wrapped around his head."

"It's because his hair fell out."

"I remember when bandits shot Reese. He had to wear a bandana." McStew grinned at the empty space between us.

And then it dawned on me about Jesse. I raced home to tell Mom. "You know how McStew has a make-believe friend?"

"That boy." Mom shook her head.

"Well, Dad has one, too."

"Oh?"

"He doesn't have any real friends, so he made one up."

Mom looked at me strangely. "Now, how can you say your father doesn't have any friends?"

"Well, *I've* never seen him with anybody."

"He has you," my mother reminded me. "You're real."

But the next day something happened to change my mind about Jesse being make-believe. When I got home from school, Dad was hosing down the tree. I walked up behind him and was about to speak when I heard him say, "The sky's the limit. I'll take you anywhere, just say the word." At first I thought he meant the tree, but then he said, "Jesse. My love. Come back to me."

"Dad?"

He turned and squirted me with the hose. Mom came rushing out and took it away from him. "Come on, Frank. Come inside."

He said, "But Audrey—"

"Audrey's fine, dear," she told him. "Everything's fine. Let's go get something to eat." She slipped her hand into his and spoke over her shoulder. "Scotty, turn off that water."

I was busy remembering something, something I'd seen in the tree a thousand times but never thought much about. After shutting off the water, I climbed into the branches to the place where Dad's tree house used to be. There, carved in the bark so I could barely see it, was a ragged-looking heart, and inside the heart were two letters, "F & J." Frank and—Jesse? The palms of my hands turned sweaty.

Who was Jesse?

I slid down the tree and heard digging sounds coming

from next door. I pushed through the hedge and there was McStew, dressed like a pirate and burying his mother's ironing board.

"Yo, mate, give me a hand." He pointed with his shovel at some bottles on the ground marked "gin." He said, "Reese got 'em when he plundered Captain Blackheart's ship, *The Bloody Bones*."

"My dad's in love with someone who's not my mom," I said and sank down on my heels.

"Me, too."

"Her name's Jesse."

"The chief's daughter. I'm going to sail away with her on Blackheart's ship."

"He thinks about her all the time."

"But first I'll have to kill him."

"What?"

"Well, naturally, he'll have to die before I can sail his ship," said McStew. "Any fool can see that. But Reese and I have a plan. After he falls asleep, we'll hack him to pieces, then feed him to the sharks. Then we'll change the ship's name to *The Gypsy Bandit*. After me."

"McStew, did you hear what I said?"

"Your dad loves Jesse."

"Can you believe it?"

"I can believe anything."

Right at that moment McStew's mother called him. We couldn't see her, but we heard her voice blow through the house like an angry wind.

"Uh-oh," said McStew. "Blackheart's wench! Here, mate, hide this!" He tossed me a half-full gin bottle. "Go—run!" For some crazy reason I did what he said, but I dropped the bottle in the hedge on the way back to my yard and left it there.

My main worry was that Dad would start talking about Jesse around Mom, and Mom would figure things out. With all her other worries, she didn't need to know about *that*. At first I planned to butt in every time Dad opened his mouth, so that Jesse's name wouldn't pop out. But that was a waste, since they were together when I wasn't around. My second idea was more clever.

"Poor Dad," I said at breakfast the next day. Mom, still in her robe, dragged a butter knife across her toast. She seemed to watch me through her eyelids. "I guess on account of the brain tumor he can't keep our names straight. He calls me Joe Bob and he thinks you're Jesse."

Mom got up in slow motion, shuffled over to the sink, and rinsed out her coffee cup. "He had a rough night," she said in a voice stuffed in cotton. "I don't imagine he'll stay home much longer . . . Scotty, you'd better spend as much time with him as you can."

I picked up my book bag. When I left the room, Mom was leaning on the sink and her shoulders were shaking. I wasn't sure whether to cuss my father or pray for him.

But I spent more time with him, like Mom said. When he wasn't mumbling about Jesse he was jabbering in what sounded like a foreign language. From where his head rested on the pillow he could look out the window and see Audrey. That stupid kids' rhyme kept running through my head: "Frank and Jesse sitting in a tree, k-i-s-s-i-n-g." But every now and then he surprised everyone by making perfect sense. One night I was reading *The Swiss Family Robinson* out loud, stumbling over words I didn't know, when Dad opened his eyes, looked at me, and said, "Sorry about the tree house, son."

"That's all right."

"Maybe you'll build it without me."

"Maybe."

"Do you still have the plan?"

I showed him the yellow paper, which I'd been using as a bookmark. Dad smiled, then closed his eyes. The next day he went into the hospital.

The days ahead were rough on Mom. She sat in the hospital while I was at school and then took me with her again at night. Most of the time Dad didn't even know we were there. Mom sat by the bed, holding his hand and whispering in his ear. I sat on the other side, reading *The Swiss Family Robinson*, even though I was pretty sure he couldn't hear.

I always thought when it was Dad's time to go he'd sit up in bed and give a speech or say something we'd all remember, like in the movies, but he died in the middle of the night while Mom and I were home asleep.

It was May and the day of his funeral was bright and sunny. I remember all the guys from the oil company showed up in their black suits and ties, the same uniform Dad always wore. Dad's sister, Aunt Hortense (Mom called her Aunt Pretense), showed up with her fat husband, Al. Mom's brother, Uncle Don, and his wife, Sue, were there from out of state. All four of my grandparents were dead and I had no cousins, although Aunt Sue was pregnant. It was a small funeral.

Mom sat in a chair facing the grave. I stood with my hand on her shoulder. I wanted to cry but couldn't. During the preacher's eulogy, which I only half heard, I watched the faces of the ladies, trying to figure out which one was Jesse, and wondered if she even came. I finally picked out someone about Dad's age who stood off by herself, away from everyone. She wore a black veil, and as soon as the service ended, she disappeared.

During the ride home, Mom and I sat in the back of Uncle Don's Ford. Mom stared out her window and didn't speak. Aunt Sue went on and on about what a great guy Frank was. She twisted her fat belly around in the front seat to say, "He just loved you all to bits, hon. Why, I don't believe he knew there were other women on the planet—did he, Don?" Mom broke down and sobbed and in my mind I saw the carved heart with "F & J." When I looked at Mom's reflection in the glass, I knew that she saw it, too.

It wasn't until a couple of days later, after the relatives were gone, that she and I talked. We were sitting on the living-room couch with pictures of Dad spread out on the coffee table, a whole shoe box full.

"I know people who put all their reminders out of sight because it's too painful," Mom said. "Well, I won't do that. I want his memory, his spirit, to fill this place. Look at him here, Scotty—how alive and healthy."

A face a lot like my own, maybe a year or two older, smiled at me from a creased black-and-white photograph. It would've been around the time of the tree house. The time of Jesse. "I feel like I didn't know him," I whispered, holding the photograph.

Mom nodded. "He wasn't easy to know. He was intensely private, but he was a good man, in most ways."

"Most?"

"Well, like all of us, he had his flaws. I think he was far more afraid than he ever admitted," Mom said, tracing her finger around Dad's mouth in one of his army photos.

"Afraid of what? Dying?"

"Afraid of the things that were different from the things he already knew."

I thought of the lady in the black veil crying into her handkerchief. How well had Dad known *her*?

A while later I was in my room tossing things over in my mind when Mom tapped on my door. Her eyes were wet. "Just remember," she said. "We never went hungry and we never lacked for comfort. He was an excellent provider and he cared deeply for us, even though he didn't always show it. Some men have a hard time with feelings. Scotty, I know it came a little late, but the tree house was his way of making up for things. If he wasn't everything you wanted—well—life isn't perfect, and neither are we."

"Mom," I said as she was about to leave, "who was that lady at the funeral? The one standing off by herself?"

Mom looked puzzled. "One of your father's secretaries, I believe. A Miss Norway. Or Norwell."

"What's her first name?"

"I'm sure I have no idea. Why?"

The next day, while Mom was out, I called up the oil company and disguised my voice. "May I speak to Miss Norway, please?"

"I beg your pardon?" said the lady who answered.

"I'd like to talk with Miss Norway. Or Norwell. Miss *Jesse* Norway. Or Norwell."

"I'm sorry, ma'am, but we have no one here by that name."

"I'm not a ma'am, I'm a mister!" I yelled, and hung up the phone.

When I went back to school the next Monday, most of the kids treated me like they were grownups. They shook my hand, patted me on the back, and they pretty much all said the same things: "Sorry about your dad, Scotty." Some acted embarrassed and didn't talk at all, I guess because they didn't know what to say. But my teacher, Mrs. Mackley, knew what to say: "Oh, you poor child." She offered to share her lunch with me. I didn't want her lunch. I just wanted to be left alone. The one person who I hoped would say something was Lynette Stoddard. I'd had a crush on her since second grade. But Lynette just walked right by me.

Mom and I went on with things as best we could. She started looking for part-time work, even though Dad's savings and insurance policy left us with enough to live on. She said she had to keep busy. The days went by and we did the same things, went to the same places—but we never laughed.

Then one day a couple of weeks after the funeral, I was in the living room watching TV when suddenly there was a loud thump against our front door. I opened it and McStew tumbled in. He had on his cowboy outfit.

"Quick—shut the door!" he commanded, and with

the toe of his boot he kicked it shut himself. McStew leaped to his feet, drew a toy six-gun, and dropped into a crouch. "Get down. There's thirty, maybe forty of 'em. I got six or seven before they got me." He yanked an imaginary arrow out of his shoulder, but the bruise around his eye was real.

"McStew," I said.

"Here." McStew tossed me his other six-gun. "Cover the back. The trick is to stay levelheaded or we'll end up like that fool Jackson who lost his scalp," warned McStew. "We gotta hold out until Reese gets here with the cavalry. Keep your eye out for the chief. If we can pick him off, we'll be in the clear."

"McStew—"

"Watch out!" McStew tackled me around the knees and brought me crashing to the floor. The shoe box with Dad's pictures tumbled off the coffee table and scattered everywhere. "Flaming arrows—now we're in for it! Cover me while I reload. Then we'll dive through the window and make for the river!"

"Scotty, what was that loud noise?" Mom came into the room holding a pitcher of iced tea. "Oh, it's you, McStew, I should have known. You'd better run along, we're about to have dinner."

"Sure thing, ma'am." McStew touched the brim of his hat. To me he said, "See you around, Durango," and took back his six-gun. He twirled them both into their holsters and ran out the door.

Mom shook her head. "That boy, I just don't know." And we looked at each other and laughed. And we laughed, then we laughed some more, and Mom spilled some iced tea. She said, "Scotty, see if he'll come back for dinner. I doubt his mother cooks much."

I looked around outside but McStew was nowhere in sight. Mom began scooping up pictures. "Why don't you finish straightening up here while I check the stove," she said.

Out of the corner of my eye I saw Toby drag off one of the photographs.

"Hey," I said, but he slipped under the couch. "Give that back, you stupid cat!" I peeked under and saw Toby's yellow eyes peeking back. The photo dangled from his mouth. "How'd you like to be buried in Mc-Stew's back yard?" To my surprise, he dropped the card and went slinking out of the room.

The picture was of Mom and Dad when they were twelve or thirteen. They were sitting hand in hand on a corner of Dad's tree house, bare legs dangling, smiling down at the camera, which was probably held by my grandmother or grandfather. When I flipped it over, I couldn't believe my eyes. I ran into the kitchen waving the picture.

"You? *You're* Jesse?"

Mom dried her hands on her apron. "He used to call me that, yes."

"So Dad didn't have a secret girlfriend?"

"Secret girlfriend? Frank? Ha!"

"But I thought—"

Mom turned the stove down and her face grew serious. "All that was ages ago," she said.

"Why didn't you tell me?"

"Was it your business?"

"But—"

"I'll tell you this much. Your father was quite a dashing figure when we were young. Very charming, in fact."

"Dad?"

"Don't laugh. He promised to show me the world, but all I wanted was California." Mom said, "I once had a babysitter—Lily Dupont—who ran off to Paris when she was seventeen. I thought that was the most romantic thing I'd ever heard of. Frank said, 'Why stop with Paris? The sky's the limit!' And for starters, he built that tree house and called it our 'Castle in the Sky.' Now, how could I resist a boy like that?" The question wasn't meant for me. Her eyes gazed past my head and out the window at Audrey.

"But why'd he call you Jesse?"

"He said we'd be outlaws—Frank and Jesse James. Go where we wanted, do what we pleased. Live like the wind." Mom smiled. "We were very young."

"So what happened?"

She plopped down in a chair by the table. "Life is what happened. Just plain old life. He went to work for the oil company straight out of high school. The idea was, we'd save enough money to go all the places he'd planned. But the next thing I knew, the years slipped by and he stopped calling me Jesse. We never even saw California." Mom suddenly looked very tired. "People change, in time. And so do their dreams."

I said, "Know what I wish? I wish I'd played with him more."

"Oh, Scotty, you did fine. I suppose we all did, in our way," Mom said. "But as long as we're wishing, I wish I had a nice stiff drink—which is strange, because I don't drink."

"Wait right there," I said and dashed across the porch and out the screen door. When I got to the hedge I reached in and snatched out the gin bottle I'd dropped. Turning to go back, I glanced up at Audrey, whose fat green leaves swayed in the breeze. Somewhere up there my father was carving initials.

"Want to dig for treasure?" a voice called to me from over the hedge.

"Want to build a tree house?" I called back.

McStew's hat poked through. "When?"

"Day after tomorrow. Beginning of summer vacation."

"We'll be here!"

"Scott Hansen!" Mom was standing on the porch stoop. "Where did you get that?"

"You said you wanted a drink."

"Get rid of it—now!"

I handed the bottle to McStew. "Will you bury this?"

"I'll add it to my collection."

"McStew, would you like to come for dinner?" Mom asked him.

McStew tipped his hat in her direction. "Much obliged, but first I got a little business up on Boot Hill."

"Come here, Scotty," Mom said. She still held the photograph of her and Dad. A smile crept across her face when she read the words he'd scribbled on the back: "Frank and Jesse. The sky's the limit."

She put her arm around me and together we looked up at the oak, at the boy and girl sitting in its branches, holding hands, dreaming of their future.

McStew's
Last Stand

We started building the tree house in June, the first day of summer vacation. I figured with me not knowing what I was doing and McStew just getting in the way, we'd be lucky to finish by Christmas. What I didn't count on was McStew's ambition. Early that first morning he woke me up by throwing stones against my window.

"You going to sleep all day?" he shouted.

"Shh. You'll wake Mom."

The sun wasn't even out yet. I pulled on some jeans, a T-shirt, and sneakers and stumbled out to the back yard, where McStew was pacing circles around the big stack of building materials. We'd pulled the tarp off the night before and the wood was wet with dew.

"First thing we'll need's a rope ladder," said McStew. In his hand was *The Swiss Family Robinson*, which I knew he'd have trouble reading, but I'd lent it to him anyway. Chapter 9, "The Tree House," was marked with the yellow paper Dad had drawn the plan on. "I studied it good," said McStew. "Not bad for a guy with a bullet in his brain."

"Tumor," I said. "Dad had a tumor."

"Same thing."

His dad was some kind of traveling salesman who didn't stay home much. When he did come home, he beat up McStew's mother, who was usually drunk, and sometimes he even beat up McStew. Mom and I would hear him cussing and yelling and throwing furniture. Once Mom called the cops.

I should've figured from the start that McStew wasn't building the tree house just to play in. He was building it to live in. The first sign was when he stopped being fun. McStew might've been nuts, but he was always fun, pretending he and everyone else around him were something besides what they really were—cowboys, pirates, gangsters. His yard was the Bounding Main, the trees were man-eating giants, his house was Fort Apache, and he called himself the Gypsy Bandit. Then there was Reese, who never left his side. Sometimes in class the teacher would say, "McStew, who are you muttering to back there?"

At first I thought he'd be so wrapped up in his other world that we'd never get anything done, but just the opposite turned out to be true. McStew got bossy. From the start, it had to be his way or no way. It was, "Durango, do this—Durango, hand me that tape measure—Durango, go here, Durango, go there."

"My name's not Durango," I told him, but he pretended not to hear. So finally I just walked away.

I was in the kitchen gulping down the last drops of milk from a bottle when Mom walked in. "It was almost gone," I said quickly. "See?" I turned the bottle upside down.

Mom slid into a chair at the kitchen table and kicked off her shoes. She'd just gotten back from selling Avon door-to-door. It was her first job.

"So how was work?" I sat down across from her.

"Not bad if you don't mind having doors closed in your face, sometimes politely, sometimes not."

"But I thought ladies liked that stuff. Lipstick and all."

"Apparently not as much as they like their afternoon TV shows. The only person to invite me in was a man whose wife wasn't home, and I don't think he was interested in makeup . . . And look—I tore my dress getting in and out of the car."

"Aw," I said. I didn't know what else to say.

"Well, how's the tree house coming?" Mom asked.

"Don't ask."

"That bad?"

"Take a look." From where we sat at the kitchen table, we could see McStew up in the tree, swinging the hammer like he was pounding in the heads of bad guys. "No matter what I do, I'm in his way."

"Maybe it'd help if you took him some water," Mom suggested. "I'll bet he's good and thirsty."

"Nothing doing. Let him get his own water."

"Well, at least bring me some. I feel like I've crossed the Sahara."

When I climbed back up in the tree, McStew handed me a hammer as if I'd never been away. "Nail that bracket to that branch."

"Are you sure you're following my dad's plan?"

"Are you here to work or ask questions?"

"Let's not forget whose tree house this is," I said.

"That reminds me. You might have to find another tree—"

"What!"

"—if you can't take orders."

"Okay, McStew, that does it! Go home!"

"Mutiny will not be tolerated."

I kicked at him and he grabbed my leg. I held onto a branch to keep from falling, and with my other foot I kicked his ear, which started to bleed. He bit my ankle and I pulled his hair. He swung at me with the hammer, just missing my nose.

Mom hurried out with her mouth full of food. "What on earth's going on?" She shaded her eyes with a napkin.

"It's all McStew's fault," I said.

"Sorry, Mrs. Hansen." McStew wiped blood off his ear with his shirttail. "I didn't know about Scotty's dad's dying wish."

"What are you talking about?" Mom asked.

"Durango—I mean Scotty—just told me how his dad made him promise to build the tree house by himself, without any help."

"He what?"

"I never did!" I shouted. "He's lying!"

"Then he hauled off and hit me with the hammer." McStew pointed at his bloody ear.

"Francis Scott Hansen, come down here!"

"But, Mom."

"This instant!"

I picked my way down the rope ladder and followed Mom's back across the yard. To make things worse, she stepped on a sharp twig in her stocking foot and had to limp the rest of the way.

"You should be good and ashamed," she said when we were inside. "As if I don't have enough on my mind without having to come between you and your friend."

"He's not my friend."

"Then why did you ask him to build the tree house?"

"I asked him to *help*. Then he took over."

"Well, just remember—he has a tough life."

"So do I."

"Not as tough as it's going to get," said Mom, twisting her foot up in the air to see if she got a splinter. "Where's that peroxide?" Just then I heard her dress rip some more and I decided it was time to go to my room.

When I got up there, the first thing I saw was Toby, nosing around in my stuff. I picked him up by the scruff of his furry old neck. "Kitty, kitty," I said, and noticed that my bedroom window was open. Hmm, I thought. But finally I just shooed him off into the hall. Then I closed the window and turned the radio on as loud as it would go—rock and roll—to drown out the sounds of hammering.

"Why can't he build a tree house in his own back yard?" I asked at dinner.

"There aren't any trees in his back yard," Mom replied. "Just in the front."

"Some excuse." I could hear a saw being dragged back and forth across a plank of wood.

A couple of hours later I was in the living room eating ice cream and watching TV. Mom came in and said, "Don't you think it would be nice if you offered Mc-Stew some ice cream?"

"You mean he's still out there?"

"I'm sure he'd appreciate it."

"Soon as the next commercial comes on," I said, and felt her eyes drilling into my neck. "Okay, I'm going! Jeez!"

McStew had a sheet of tar paper rolled clear across our back yard. "Here—hold that section down while I cut it." As usual, he spoke to me as if I'd been there the whole time. "I just hope I measured it right. It's for the walls." He knelt down on the grass next to the tar paper with a pair of heavy scissors out of Dad's tool chest.

"How can you even see anything?" I asked, as Mc-Stew snipped away in the dark.

"Oh, crap!" He threw down the scissors. "Lucky we have five more rolls. How many tree houses was your dad planning on building, anyway?"

I went back inside. "He said he didn't want any ice cream," I told Mom.

I went to sleep to the sounds of cutting, sawing, hammering, and cussing. The next morning when I went outside, our yard looked like somebody had put it in a giant bag, shaken it up, then dumped it out again. Mc-Stew was nowhere in sight, but there were scraps of wood, pieces of tar paper, bent nails, sandpaper, hammers, a saw, scissors, and a hand drill scattered on the ground beneath the oak. It wasn't enough that his yard was messed up. He had to come over and mess up ours.

When I glanced at the huge slab of plywood nailed into the branches (the floor), I spotted one dirty sneaker and one bare foot sticking over the edge. I climbed the rope ladder and there was McStew flat on his back, asleep. Toby was stretched out next to him.

I climbed down, got my ball and mitt, and headed for Jollyman Park, thinking this might not be such a bad deal after all. I'd never wanted to build a tree house—that was Dad's idea. Now Dad was gone and here was McStew doing it all by himself. I was free to spend the summer playing ball, which is what I wanted to do all along.

But when I got home that afternoon, McStew said, "We got a problem." He was sitting at our kitchen table eating a peanut-butter-and-jelly sandwich and drinking a glass of milk. A glob of grape jelly clung to his chin.

"Why're you in our house?" I demanded.

"Before she went off to work, your mom said I could fix a sandwich."

I yanked open the refrigerator door and snatched out a bottle of milk.

"She told me to tell you to use a glass," said McStew with his mouth full.

"How about going and eating that in your own house?" I said.

"Don't you want to hear our problem?"

"No."

"We don't have any paint. It's the one thing your dad forgot."

"So?"

"Paint protects wood. I was thinking green would be

good. It'll hide the house from pirates, bandits, and Indians."

"McStew, there aren't any pirates, bandits, or Indians."

"That's what you think."

"Well, I guess you'll just have to get by without it."

"Old Man Miller has a whole shed full," said McStew. "I saw it. Some of it's green."

"Oh, and you think he'll hand it over? Old Man Miller's the stingiest guy in the neighborhood. And he hates kids. Everybody knows that."

"Actually, I was thinking we could sneak over one night and help ourselves," said McStew, wiggling his eyebrows.

"That's stealing."

He licked peanut butter off his thumb.

"Forget it," I said. "You're crazy. And know what else? You and your stupid tree house can rot, for all I care. I'm not forgetting that lie you told."

"What lie?"

"Telling my mom what I said Dad's last words were."

"Well, what were they, then?"

"How should I know? I wasn't there," I said

"So those could've been his last words, right?" McStew asked.

"I don't want to talk about it."

"I wish I knew *my* dad's last words."

"Your dad's not dead."

"It'd still be great to hear them." McStew dipped two fingers deep into the jar of peanut butter and stuck them in his mouth.

"That's disgusting," I said. "If my mom saw you do that . . ."

He got up from the table, leaving his dirty plate and glass. He said, "Which way's the washing machine? She told me I could put these in." He held up the filthy shirt and jeans he'd worn for the last several days.

I grabbed them away from him. "Go back to your tree. I'll put them in."

"Easy on the starch," said McStew. He went out through the back porch, and I noticed for the first time that he was wearing *my clothes*.

In the garage, I flung open the lid of the washing machine and saw that Mom had detergent and a load of things ready to go. I guess she was just waiting for McStew's stuff. They were stiff and stinky and I thought it would be better just to burn them. I threw them in the machine, thinking I'd have to boil my hands to get them clean. I was so mad I wanted to kick something. As luck would have it, Toby walked by. I don't know what made me do it, but I picked him up and put him in the washing machine and lowered the lid. I had no intention of leaving him there, but it was either that or run wild in the streets. I held my ear to the lid, waiting to hear him meow for help, then I'd rescue him.

The phone rang, making me jump, as if whoever was calling was a spy. I ran to answer it, hoping it would be one of my friends, but it was some guy wanting to talk to Mom. Right after I hung up, she came staggering through the front door the way McStew did when he pretended to be shot full of arrows.

"Somewhere there's a better life," Mom groaned.

"I'm thirty-two going on seventy. It's Death Valley out there." Her makeup was smeared and sweaty-looking; makeup was what she sold door-to-door.

"You just got a message," I said. "It's by the phone."

"If there's a God in heaven it's about a new job. Scotty, be a lifesaver and get me some lemonade."

I saw her pat her hairdo on her way to the phone. When I got back with the lemonade, she was nodding and going, "Uh-huh, uh-huh— Oh, absolutely, I certainly can, oh, yes, you bet."

While she was talking, someone knocked on the front screen door. I was surprised to see Mrs. Stewart, McStew's mother, standing on our porch stoop. She had on the black-and-blue checkered dress, and for a second I thought she'd ask me to put it in the washing machine with McStew's stuff. She was carrying a rabbit, of all things. The rabbit was scrawny and dirty. It had one bent ear and a missing eye. McStew's mother had missing teeth. She stood there running her fingers through the rabbit's fur. I noticed that her nails looked cracked and bleedy.

"Sorry to be a bother, Frank," she spoke in a loud voice. "Is my boy here?"

"Scotty," I said. "My name's Scotty. Frank was my dad."

"And I'd like to state how sorrowful I am over his passing," said Mrs. Stewart. "The neighborhood's not the same without him. I've been meaning to bake you and your sister a fruit pie but we've fallen on hard times at our place and I don't know what'll come of it, I really don't."

"He's in the back yard," I said.

"Your father?"

"Your son."

Did I imagine it, or could I smell her through the screen?

Just then Mom came skipping up, all smiles. "Hi! You're looking at the new phone receptionist at Pinky's Auto Parts! Won't you please come in?"

"Mom," I said, giving her a look.

"Scotty, go get another glass of lemonade," Mom ordered.

"Oh, hon, I don't drink lemonade," said Mrs. Stewart with her face pressed against the screen. "I was just explaining to"—she nodded at me—"how sorrowful I am over your father's passing. I've been meaning to bake you two a fruit pie."

"My father?"

"She thinks you're my sister." I rolled my eyes.

"Why, you sweet woman! Are you sure you won't come in?"

"Thank you, no," answered Mrs. Stewart. The whole while she talked, she was petting the rabbit. Clumps of fur floated down around the toes of her scuffed shoes. "I came over on account of"—her eyes dropped to the rabbit—"I thought you might like to keep him."

For the first time, Mom noticed the animal, which looked like it might drop dead at any moment.

"We already have a cat," I said. "We don't need a rabbit."

"Oh, hon, I don't mean little Pussywillow here, no, no—he was a gift." Mrs. Stewart hugged her rabbit. "I was referring to my boy. Mick."

"What!" Mom and I said together.

"He's better off with you, anyone can see that. And like I said, we've got hard times at our place. Mick's father"—Mrs. Stewart stopped for a breath—"is away a lot and I got reason to suspect he's not coming home. It's hard on a woman, and, well, if I could just speak to your mother—"

"Mrs. Stewart, I *am* Scotty's mother. Now, what's this foolishness about giving away your son?"

"I love him. I do. It's just that I can't do for him no more. Look at me. I can't hardly do for myself. And what with his father gone—well, I got reason to believe he's up and took himself another wife," Mrs. Stewart whispered through the screen, as if she didn't want the neighbors to hear.

"Oh, he can't do that while he's married to you," Mom pointed out.

"You don't know the son of a bitch! He was wed to two others when he wed me. Swore I'd be the last. Liar!"

"I don't believe I can listen to any more of this," said Mom.

"Well, you give it some thought," said Mrs. Stewart, taking a step back. "I'm sure you'll come to a wise decision, based on—" She didn't finish. "In the meantime, I'll bake you that fruit pie. I might be moving."

After she left, Mom stood staring at the rabbit fur on our door mat. "I think I'm going to be ill," she said.

"If you think you're ill now, wait until you taste that fruit pie," I told her.

"You know something? It should be illegal for some people to have children. And who in their right mind gave that woman a rabbit?" I stood by and watched her get angrier by the moment. "Scotty, bring me the phone directory. I'm going to call the health department, or child welfare—or something. This can't go on." She flipped through the phone book, then suddenly snapped it shut. "Oh, Lord, they'll probably stick him in an orphanage."

"What's wrong with that?"

"Would you say that if it was *you*? Well, I won't let it happen," Mom said before I could answer. "We'll do what that so-called mother of his said. We'll keep him."

"We'll what?"

"The first chance you get, Scotty, I want you and McStew to go over there and rescue that rabbit. We'll keep him, too."

"Why don't we just keep the whole family?" I complained, but she was already on her way out back to talk to McStew.

That evening McStew sat across from me at the dinner table.

"Boy, am I lucky or what," he said, grinning. Grease from a chicken leg dripped down his chin. In his other hand was a corncob, bright with butter. "Suddenly I got three homes, all of them next door to each other. One I even built myself. One wall's a little crooked, but it'll be good for draining rain off." Mom kept piling his plate high with food and McStew kept making it disappear.

"I wonder if *I* could have a little of that?" I grumbled.

"Are your arms painted on?" said Mom. "Help yourself."

"I can't wait to start on the roof," said McStew, licking his fingers. "Castle in the Sky!"

"What? What did you say?" Mom stared at him.

"It's what's written on the plan Scotty's dad made," McStew explained. "Castle in the Sky. Neat name, huh?" He stuffed his face with corn bread and mumbled, "Home of the Gypsy Bandit."

Mom sucked in her bottom lip and rested a hand on McStew's shoulder. It was more than I could take. I was about to hurl mashed potatoes in his face when I heard something that made me sick to my stomach.

"What's that?" I asked.

"What's what?" said Mom.

"That noise! Listen."

"You mean the washing machine?"

"The washing machine! The washing machine!"

"Scotty, sit down. What ails you?"

"Did you look inside before you turned it on?" I asked.

"I didn't have to," Mom answered. "The clothes and detergent were already in there and McStew tells me you put in his shirt and trousers. If there's something you want washed, you'll just have to wait."

"Nothing like clean duds," said McStew, cheeks bulging.

I excused myself, saying I had to use the bathroom. When I got to the garage, the washing machine was churning away. It had already gone into "spin" and I imagined our clothes and stuff zooming around at an enormous speed along with Toby the cat. And then, while I stood there, it stopped. I wasn't sure what to do. I didn't want to deal with a dead cat, but I didn't want

Mom to find him either. I sucked in my breath and with shaky fingers started to lift the lid.

"I thought you said you were going to use the bathroom." The sound of Mom's voice made me drop the lid.

"Oh—hi, Mom."

"I didn't know we *had* a bathroom out here." She narrowed her eyes and I just shrugged. "Suppose you stop acting rude and go have dessert with your friend."

"I'll be right in. I'm looking for my—my—"

"Well, whatever it is, look for it later. Now, go on while I put this wash in the dryer. You and McStew clean up the kitchen when you finish—do you hear?"

I dragged my feet back to the kitchen. All the dirty dishes were still on the table and McStew was gone. I spotted him through the window, about to climb the rope ladder. I wasted no time getting out there.

"McStew—I'm running away and I need Dad's plan!"

"Fat chance."

"But you're nearly done here, and I've got to go build my own tree house in some other state."

"Come on up," he said.

"I don't have time. Just hand over the plan." But McStew was on his way up the ladder. I watched the house for Mom to come charging out with a posse of policemen, then I climbed up, too. And that's when I got the surprise of my life. For there was Toby, safe and sound, curled up in a gray ball on the floor of the tree house.

"Friend of yours?" said McStew, running his hand through the cat's fur.

I felt so overjoyed I tried giving Toby a hug, but he hissed, arched his back, and leaped out of the tree.

"Guess not," said McStew.

"But how—"

"Funny thing. After you took my shirt and jeans I remembered I had some socks that needed washing. I got them out of here and went around the side of the house to the garage. And you'll never guess who I found in the washing machine."

"Oh, man! You saved my life," I told him.

"I saved Toby's life. You could still die."

"What do you mean?"

"I mean I could tell your mom."

"Why would you want to do that?"

"I didn't say I wanted to. I said I *could*. But then again, maybe I won't—if you get that paint."

"What paint?"

"You know what paint."

"Aw, jeez."

"Three or four buckets ought to be enough."

"I won't do it."

"And paint thinner—don't forget the paint thinner."

"McStew—"

Mom's voice called to us from the back porch. "You boys come down here and wash these dinner dishes!"

"Mrs. Hansen, I have some big news for you," McStew called back.

"Okay, dammit, I'll do it," I said.

"*What* news?" said Mom.

"That was the best meal I've eaten in five years," McStew said, but it was me he was grinning at.

"I'm glad you enjoyed it, but you still have to wash the dishes."

Late that night, after Mom thought I was asleep, I sneaked out to the oak tree. McStew said I should wear something dark, so I had on a black sweater, black ski pants, and a black wool cap of my dad's.

"What a great getup," McStew said when he saw me. "I wish I looked like that."

"I'm going to sweat to death! Listen, McStew, I just thought of something. My mom will *buy* you paint if that's what you want. All we have to do is ask her."

McStew looked disappointed. "Sometimes, Durango, I just don't know." Then he said, "Okay, here's what. You know where Old Man Miller's house is, right? There's an alley out back. Stick close to the fences and trees. The shed isn't lit, it's totally dark, I checked it out myself. There's a latch on the door, so you'll need this." He showed me a file from my dad's tool chest. "All you need is to pry it a little and it'll snap right open. Here's a flashlight."

"Aren't you coming?"

"I wish I could. You know how I love an adventure. But since Reese and I did all the work on the tree house, we figured it's your turn to do something. Right, Reese?"

"But how do you know Old Man Miller even *has* green paint?" I asked.

"Oh, he has it, all right, I counted four half-gallon cans. And you might as well get them all."

"So if you were in there, why didn't you just grab them yourself?"

"I didn't want you accusing me of doing your job," he said.

"McStew, one of these days I'm going to kill you."

"Hear that, Reese? Sounds like another bounty hunter— Don't forget the paint thinner. And, oh yeah, some paintbrushes."

"This is blackmail," I said, and made my way down the ladder.

I'd never been so scared in my life. Sneaking through people's back yards and alleys and plastering myself against the sides of houses whenever headlights came in sight—I felt like all the criminals I'd seen in all the movies I'd watched. And I *was* a criminal. I'd nearly murdered my mother's cat. If it wasn't for McStew, Toby would be dead for sure. Well, I'd learned my lesson. I thought, just let me get out of this one and I'll be an animal lover for life. Especially cats. I'll even adopt Mrs. Stewart's rabbit if I have to. Just so long as I don't have to adopt McStew.

There were five blocks between the Miller house and ours. They seemed like five miles. The lock on the shed snapped open just as McStew said it would. The inside smelled musty and damp like old burlap. Using the flashlight, I found the green paint and started back, a half-gallon bucket in each hand. Every so often I had to set them down and wipe sweat out of my eyes. I stuck close to the alleys.

"Wow, you made it!" McStew slapped me on the back. "Anybody shoot at you?"

I handed him the file, which I'd tucked into the waist of my ski pants.

He said, "Better keep that for a weapon. Word's out that Blackheart's pirate crew is roaming the streets seeking revenge for his death. A while ago I saw two guys hanging from street lamps. You don't want to join them, do you? Reese and I will guard the fort."

"McStew," I said, shaking my fist.

On my second trip a cop car nearly caught me in the beam of its headlights and I dove into some bushes. My heartbeat was so loud I'm surprised he didn't stop to investigate. A while later a teenager stepped out of a garage, smoking a cigarette. "Who you s'posed to be, kid? Batman?"

"Zorro," I answered.

He laughed and held out his cigarette. "Smoke?"

"Maybe later." I kept walking.

"Hey, whatcha got in those buckets?" he called after me.

"Homework." I turned down a different alley.

When I got back to the tree house, I said, "Some guy saw me. He saw the paint, too."

McStew said a cuss word. "Spies are everywhere."

"Well, anyway, this should do it." I was sweating enough to fill all four buckets.

"Um—paint thinner?" McStew reminded me.

"Like I said, I'm going to kill you."

The scariest part was when I was inside Old Man Miller's shed. I was afraid he'd hear me or see the flashlight. Except for cookies in the school cafeteria, I'd never stolen anything. I wondered how many years behind bars I could get for this.

"Pirates tried taking over the fort," said McStew

when I got back with the paint thinner. "But don't worry, Reese killed two and I killed five. The rest ran off. Blackheart is unavenged!"

"Well, I hope you're satisfied," I said, pulling off my wool cap.

McStew looked around. "Paintbrushes?"

"Give me a break!"

"What are we supposed to paint with, our toes?"

"The shed was fresh out of paintbrushes—I looked."

"Try looking in a can on the shelf above your head to the right when you first go in the door"—McStew grinned—"and you'll see the paintbrushes."

I just groaned.

"And see if you can grab an empty bucket to mix this stuff in. You're a good man, Durango. Reese says I should promote you."

By the time I'd made my last trip, I felt like *I* was Old Man Miller, tired, sore, bent over, and grumpy. But McStew treated me like a hero. "Four times without getting caught! Someday they'll write a song about you."

"I'm going to bed," I said.

"Aw, come on. Stick around. We'll sing pirate songs."

"You die at dawn!"

It took all the strength I had just to pull off my sweater and ski pants. I dropped them into a bucket on the back porch and tiptoed up to my room. I don't even remember hitting the mattress.

"Scotty—wake up!" My mother was calling me from somewhere far away. When I opened my eyes, the room was full of sunlight and Mom's frowning face was staring down at me. "Why are you still in bed? It's nearly noon."

I squinted against the light, stretched, and yawned. "I thought you started your new job today."

"I did, but I had to hurry home. Won't that look nice on my record! Now get dressed and come right down," she ordered. "We have company." Then she went away.

Suddenly I remembered about last night.

I leaped out of bed and into my clothes. Downstairs were voices I didn't recognize. I took one step of the stairs at a time, like someone easing into shark-filled waters. Sitting on the edge of the couch, hunched over his knobby cane like a leftover Halloween costume, was Old Man Miller. A man in a black business suit was talking to my mom. And a neighbor, Mr. Ramsey from up the street, stood close by. They all got quiet when they saw me.

"Come here, son," said the man in the suit. "I'd like to ask you some questions." He looked like the warden in all those prison movies I'd seen, the guy who always made sure you got to the electric chair on time. Even James Cagney couldn't get away from him. He was the last guy I wanted to talk to. "For starters, what can you tell me about these?" He held up my black sweater and ski pants.

I opened my mouth but all that came out was a squeak of air.

"Scotty, answer the gentleman," said Mom. Her voice sounded shaky.

"They're my, my—" I said.

The man in the suit held on to the clothes as if they were murder weapons.

Mr. Ramsey stepped forward. "Scotty—I saw you last night." He glanced with worried eyes at my mother. The Ramseys had been at my dad's funeral. "You were in the alley behind my house. You were wearing—" He nodded at the clothes in the Warden's hand. "And you were carrying buckets of paint."

"*My* paint," snarled Old Man Miller, staring at the floor.

"What paint do you mean?" I managed to ask.

"Now, son, think before you speak," said the man in the suit. I didn't like his tone, which was low and quiet. I didn't like anything about him, and I hated it when people called me "son." "We found it out back in the tree. Four cans."

"And thinner!" Old Man Miller's teeth clacked together. "Mine!"

Mom began to cry. The palms of my hands were wet. I stuffed them under my armpits.

For a moment nobody acted as if they knew what to do. Then the man in charge said, "Sorry for the inconvenience, ma'am, but we're going to have to ask you and your son to accompany us down to the precinct." My knees began to wobble and I felt as if I was going to throw up. A patrol car was parked out front. A policeman leaned against the hood. Some kids and grownups had gathered on the sidewalk.

I dropped flat on my butt on the bottom step. When the man in the suit reached out for me, I held my wrists up for the handcuffs, but all he did was pull me to my feet.

Someone, Mr. Ramsey I think, helped Old Man Miller up and we all went outside. I could feel Mom walking behind me but I couldn't make myself look at her. All I wanted right then was a newspaper to cover my face.

We were partway down the walk when a voice behind us said, "You got the wrong man, Sheriff! I'm the one you want!" It was McStew. He must've been in the kitchen listening to us the whole time.

"How's that?" The man in the suit looked annoyed. He had taken out a cigarette the moment he left the house but hadn't lit it yet.

"*I* took that paint," said McStew, and I heard Mom gasp.

"And thinner!" said Old Man Miller.

"Yeah, that, too," said McStew.

"Don't make no never mind who took it." Old Man Miller leaned himself against Mr. Ramsey with one hand and waved his cane with the other. "It's still mine!"

"Who are *you*?" asked the Warden in that same low voice.

"He's our next-door neighbor," Mom answered at the same time McStew said, "The Gypsy Bandit." "His name is Mick Stewart."

"Don't you fret, ma'am," McStew told her. "This day was bound to come."

"Now, let me get this straight," said the man. "Are you saying *you* stole the paint from this gentleman's property?"

"With a little help from Reese." McStew nodded. "But don't think you're going to catch *him*. He set sail on Blackheart's ship at dawn."

"Wait a minute here," said Mr. Ramsey. "I saw Scotty with my own eyes—"

"What you saw was me in Durango's clothes," Mc-Stew told him. "I'm wearing his duds right now. See? We're the same size."

For a few moments everyone looked McStew and me up and down as if we were about to try on some clothes. Then McStew said, "It's like this, Sheriff. My pard here tried talking sense into me, but when he wasn't looking I snuck into his room and helped myself to that getup you're holding. After everyone was asleep, that's when I made my move."

"Oh, McStew!" said Mom.

"Fact is, I'd've been in the badlands of New Mexico by now, but I can't let another man swing for my crime—so take me away." He held out his wrists just as I'd done.

"Who did you say this boy was?" the Warden asked my mother.

"Mick Stewart. He lives over there."

"Go get his parents," the man ordered the cop, who went, without speaking, to our neighbors' door.

By now it seemed like half the neighborhood was standing around. It took several minutes, but Mrs. Stewart finally came to the door. She was holding her rabbit. The cop tried his best to get her to come out, but she wouldn't budge from behind the screen. I heard her mutter something about a "conspiracy." Even Mom couldn't persuade Mrs. Stewart to go with her son to the police precinct. I watched the two men help McStew into the back of the patrol car, minus handcuffs.

"Don't worry about me," he spoke out the window. "The prison's not built that can hold the Gypsy Bandit."

McStew's mother still stood in her doorway staring out at the empty street after the patrol car took away her son.

"Mrs. Stewart," Mom called to her. "Would you care to come over and sit with us?" But she wouldn't answer. She only stood and stared. "That poor woman," Mom whispered. "That poor family."

"What about my paint?" growled Old Man Miller. "And my thinner?"

"Don't worry, you'll get it," Mr. Ramsey promised him. "The police took it for evidence."

"I'll sue!" Old Man Miller glared at Mr. Ramsey as if *he'd* stolen the paint, and for a minute I thought he was going to smack him with his cane.

Mom said, "Scotty, I'm going to drive down to the precinct. I just can't let that poor boy go through this ordeal without at least one friendly face." Then she spoke to Mrs. Murton, our nosy neighbor from across the street. "Would you mind if Scotty stayed with you until I get back?"

"Oh, certainly, certainly." Mrs. Murton tried to put her arm around me, but I wasn't about to stay with her. I wanted to go sit in the tree house.

After Mom drove off, one of the neighborhood kids called to me as I headed toward the back yard, "Hey, Scotty! Who'd McStew kill, anyway?"

Two days later there was an article in the morning newpaper which Mom read out loud. It talked about Mick Stewart's "sad home life and bereft mother," whom the cops came back to question twice. McStew's father, a salesman, "was presumably out of state, where-abouts unknown." The article went on to say how

McStew had been living in a tree house in a neighbor's yard and how he'd "come forth to confess to a prankish stunt thought to have been committed by a friend." I was grateful that they didn't print the friend's name.

"Prankish stunt," said Mom with a smile. "Not 'crime,' but 'prankish stunt.' Can you imagine how many people will read this and think what I'm thinking?"

I asked her what she was thinking.

"That here's a boy worth saving."

That night I poked my head into Mom's room. She was propped up in bed reading a book, as she always did before going to sleep. Toby was snoozing at her side.

"McStew didn't steal that paint," I said quickly. "I did." Then I went to my room and crawled under the covers to wait for the cops. Pretty soon I heard Mom's slippers slapping down the hall. She stood in the doorway.

"Yes, I know," she said, then returned to her room.

The next day at breakfast I said, "*How* did you know?"

"I'm your mother. I know."

"Then why did you let them take McStew away instead of—instead of me?"

She squinted at me over her coffee cup. "A better question might be, why did *you* let them take McStew away?"

"I was scared," I answered and felt my cheeks grow warm.

"So did you think that if you told me, I'd fix everything?"

"No. I just—I don't know."

"Well"—Mom sighed—"I'm afraid this is something you're going to have to work out for yourself. And as for McStew, I'm sure he did exactly what he wanted to do. After all, he enjoys putting on a show."

"Are you saying he *wanted* to go to jail?"

Mom laughed. "Scotty, McStew's not in jail. He's probably sitting somewhere having a bigger breakfast than we are."

"How do you know?"

"I've made a few calls," she said. "He's fine. He'll most likely be adjudicated a ward of the state and go to a foster home. I admit I had some doubts about what would happen if the authorities got hold of him, but he's surely better off with them than he was next door. And something else. Wherever that boy lands, he'll land on his feet." She took a sip of coffee and gazed out the window at the tree house.

Part of me wanted to shake McStew's hand and another part wanted to push him out a window, just to see if he *would* land on his feet. He was a hero and I wasn't. He was someone not afraid to make things happen, and I was someone who stood by while things happened around me. I was just a kid living with his mother and whose father had died. No wonder Lynette Stoddard never spoke to me. Why should she?

"Here's an idea—" Mom tuned in on my thoughts. "The tree house isn't finished. You'll feel better if you have something to keep you busy this summer. I think we might even arrange to *buy* you some paint."

Shortly after that, McStew's mother moved out of

their house, leaving behind some empty gin bottles, a dead rabbit, and not much else. The rabbit stank up the neighborhood. It smelled bad enough for ten rabbits. Even after some workers came, there was still that smell.

It took me most of the summer to finish building the tree house. All it needed was a roof, the one thing Mc-Stew didn't get around to, and some paint. Luckily, he left behind Dad's plan, and after eight or nine tries I got it done. Maybe I wasn't a hero, but I did get the roof on. There were some afternoons when I'd sit in the tree house eating Oreo cookies and reading *The Swiss Family Robinson* with the rain pouring down around me. I stayed dry because I'd covered the roof with enough tar paper to keep out a tidal wave.

Somewhere, I thought, my dad is smiling.

Lynette

"Slide, Scotty!"

Those words rang in my ears as I slammed into the third baseman. We tumbled into the foul zone, heads knocking, knees bleeding.

"Safe!" shouted the umpire, and my team cheered.

"Safe, my butt!" Bobby Pike, the third baseman, spit on the ground.

"Man, when you going to learn how to slide?" said Corky Perkins after Ross Hooker hit me home.

"Any day now," I answered.

They all knew that sliding was my weak point. We won, 13–11, but I was in no mood to celebrate. After the game I went up to the umpire, a beefy-looking eighth-grader, and said, "That call you made? I should've been out."

"Don't sweat it, kid. That one was for McStew." He patted me on the shoulder.

But Bobby Pike, no McStew fan, said, "Hansen, you stink."

I dragged my feet out of Jollyman Park. "Way to go, Scotty!" someone shouted, but I didn't look back.

When I got home, Mom asked me, "Oh, my, who did *that* to you?"

"McStew," I said, and climbed the stairs to my room.

When school had let out in June, everyone acted sorry because my dad had died. Faces turned serious, as if it were bad manners to smile around me. By September, I was the most popular kid in the sixth grade, and all because of McStew. Ever since he got hauled off in a police car in front of my house, people bugged me with questions like, "Who was he, *really*?" Everyone had heard how he came to my rescue and admitted to stealing paint out of Old Man Miller's shed.

All through grade school, McStew was mostly "that weird kid" who sat in the back of the class snoozing, looking at comics, or whispering to his make-believe friend. He never bothered anybody. In fact, he hardly ever paid attention to people, and so kids left him alone. It isn't fun making fun of somebody who doesn't know you're there. Even Corky Perkins, who *loved* poking fun, never bothered McStew. The teachers got so they let him be, too. I remember once they asked Mrs. Stewart to come in for a conference to talk about what McStew's problem might be, why he always looked dirty, why he was on free lunch year after year, and why he sometimes had a black eye. I don't know what happened, but after she left the conference I don't think they ever asked her back again.

Now McStew was gone, and kids treated him like a

hero. Since I was his neighbor, the one in whose back yard he'd built a tree house, they treated me that way, too. By mid-October, I'd had enough.

"Is it true he buried stolen property in his yard?"

"All he buried was his mom's toaster and iron and stuff so she wouldn't hurt herself," I tried to explain for the hundredth time.

"But didn't he live in your tree?"

I had to admit that, yeah, that part was true.

"And didn't he rob from the rich and give to the poor?"

"Jeez," I said.

McStew's so-called fame spread to the junior high school, where some of my classmates' brothers and sisters went, like that eighth-grade umpire.

"I'm sick of McStew," I said to my mother at dinner. "I'm more sick of him now than when I had to look at him every day."

"Scotty, did anyone ever tell you you complain too much?" Mom asked. She'd had another rough day at work.

I told her, "At least I'm not the one always quitting my job."

"You're a sixth-grader. You can't quit. And, anyway, the jobs I get hurt my feet."

"What about the one at Pinky's Auto Parts? All you did was sit around answering phones."

"The people who called in were cranky. They complained too much. Remind you of anyone?"

"So now you're working at Mac's Diner. They don't complain there?"

"They complain everywhere. It's what people do," said my mother. "But at least I get tips."

The next morning on the school playground, two fifth-grade girls skipped up to me and said, "We heard McStew escaped from jail and is panning gold in Alaska." Later in the cafeteria Reggie Bryson told me that McStew had stowed away on a banana boat headed for South America.

After school I didn't walk through Jollyman Park, as I usually did, because I didn't want to run into anyone who might want to talk about *that person*. When I got home, Chip Keller was waiting for me on the front doorstep. Chip and I were in the same grade.

Before he could get a word out, I said, "I can't talk right now." He followed me into the house, uninvited.

"I have a brainstorm you'll thank me for until your dying day," said Chip. "We'll be millionaires!"

Everything Chip thought about had to do with making money. His dad was a hot-shot Cadillac man who owned the town's biggest dealership. Chip wanted to be like him, only richer.

I said, "This doesn't have anything to do with a certain somebody, does it?" I went into the kitchen with Chip tagging behind.

"Got any soda? I'm dying of thirst." He reached into the refrigerator and helped himself to a Coke. "Where's your bottle opener?"

"Listen, Chip, I have to walk to Mac's Diner. My mom's on shift and I get to eat."

"Sounds great! But I'll have to call home."

"I never said—"

But he was already dialing.

Chip never stopped talking all the way to Mac's

Diner, nine blocks away. I had dinner there twice a week and rode home with Mom when she got off at six-thirty. I liked the food at Mac's, especially the milk shakes. But today I wished I'd ridden my bike. We could've put it in the trunk of Mom's car and I wouldn't have had to listen to Chip.

"My dad says when a product's hot, that's when you should sell." He skipped a couple of steps ahead of me. "Right now, what's hot? McStew! His name's on everyone's lips. But that won't last."

"Let's hope not."

"So what we'll do," said Chip, whirling around and walking backwards in front of me, "we'll charge people to see the tree house where he lived."

"We'll what?"

"But first we need to fan the flames. People have all these wild ideas about what he was like, so let's build on that." Now Chip was walking right beside me, practically with his arm around my shoulders.

"What the heck are you talking about?" I said.

"Scotty, don't you get it? What's important here is what people *think*. Our job is to figure out what image appeals to them, and that's the one we sell. It's called creative advertising."

"Do me a favor," I said. "Don't talk about this stuff in front of my mom. Don't even talk to *me* about it."

When we got to the diner, there was Mom hustling around in her stiff green uniform, her dark hair pulled back in a bun, very un-Mom-like.

"Well, look who's here," she said. "How are you, Chip?"

"Scotty invited me."

"He invited himself," I said.

We settled into a booth and Mom took out her pad. "So what'll you boys have?"

"Can we start with chocolate shakes?" I asked.

We both ordered the Cheeseburger Deluxe with extra fries. After the food came, Chip leaned toward me like he was planning a robbery. "Okay, the biggest story around school is that McStew took from the rich and gave to the poor. Like Robin Hood."

"But he didn't."

"Duh! How many times've I got to tell you? It's what people *think* that counts. From now on, when someone asks you about McStew, that's what you say—that he snuck around at night, all dressed in black, stealing people's jewels and stuff and dropping it off at the poor-house."

"Know what? You're as bad as he is. Maybe worse." I shoved a french fry in my mouth. "Not only that, I think you're the one spreading all these stories about him. Am I right?"

Chip made sure no one was looking. Then he slipped a notebook under the table to me. I glanced at the first page. " 'The Legend of the Gypsy Bandit,' " I read out loud.

He snatched the notebook back. "Why don't you just shout it out to the whole world next time?"

"Oh, like anybody cares."

"Scotty, I can't do this without you," Chip said.

"You mean you can't do it without my tree house."

"Got any dimes? Let's play the jukebox, so people won't hear that loud voice of yours."

A box was at our table. Chip stuck in two of my dimes and pressed buttons without looking at the selections. "Jailhouse Rock" came on.

"That's where I'll end up if I listen to you," I said.

"If we do this right, kids'll line up in your yard as far as the eye can see."

"My mom will love that."

"We'll do it while she's at work."

"Then you better hurry. She could quit any minute."

After we'd eaten, Mom came over. "Would you two like some pie?"

"Not me," I said. "I'm full."

"Me, too," said Chip. "So I'll have mine to go. Cherry'll be fine."

Just then Chip's next selection started to play, and Mom sucked in her bottom lip and hurried off to the kitchen. It was a Frank Sinatra record that she and Dad used to play. It was "their" song.

"So why's she so upset?" Chip asked. "Did they run out of cherry?"

"Shut up, Chip. You don't know everything."

Mom drove us home. Chip talked the whole way but didn't mention "the plan." When we stopped in front of his house, which looked like it was the size of two houses, he handed me the notebook again. "Here's that math assignment you wanted, Scotty. I'll talk to you about it tomorrow. 'Night, Mrs. Hansen. Thanks for the lift. Oh, and by the way, I think I hear a tick in your transmission. If you want, I'll talk to my dad about getting you a good trade-in."

"What a piece of work," Mom said after Chip went

inside. Then she turned to me and asked, "Why did he give you an assignment? Weren't you in school today?"

"Of course," I answered. "It's just that—well, Chip's a real math whiz and he's been helping me study."

"Well, what do you know about that," Mom said. She looked at the Keller house and nodded her approval.

The last thing I did before going to sleep was glance over Chip's notebook—"The Legend of the Gypsy Bandit."

According to Chip, McStew was kidnapped by Gypsies when he was a baby. The Gypsies planned to take him to Europe to raise as their own, but one of them got shot in the toe by an FBI agent. They dropped him off in a bar before escaping on a shrimp boat. McStew was found by the drunken Mrs. Stewart, who named him Mick after a murdered lover, who was the reason she drank so much.

As soon as he was old enough (fourth grade), he began carrying out his lifelong plan to help poor orphans like himself. With the aid of his comical sidekick and trusty next-door neighbor (me), he went to school by day and was a burglar by night, breaking into rich people's houses and helping himself to whatever he could find, then leaving the loot in the mailboxes of orphanages. Just in case the law got wise, he built a tree house in the comical sidekick's back yard to use as a hideout. The sidekick was the only one who knew, and it was he who gave McStew his black burglar outfit.

Chip went on to write how everything was going just fine until the cops found the burglar outfit one day while McStew was off fishing, along with some green paint stolen from Old Man Miller's shed. The paint was supposed to hide the tree from McStew's enemies (that part was true). The cops were getting ready to drag the comical sidekick, who was kicking and screaming, away in handcuffs when suddenly who but McStew himself leaped out of nowhere and confessed that he was the Gypsy Bandit. "I can't let another man swing for my crime," were the last words anyone heard him say. He was put in chains and driven away in an armored car.

"To be continued," Chip had written.

It was the silliest thing I'd ever read. It had everything but a soundtrack.

When I showed up at school the next day, Chip was waiting on the playground. He was all smiles.

"Did you read it? What did you think?"

I tossed him the notebook. "Forget it."

"What do you mean, forget it? It's a masterpiece!"

"Why did you say I was kicking and screaming? You weren't even there."

"I wanted to give you an exciting scene."

"And something else—I'm not anybody's comical side-kick!"

"Okay, so I'll cross those parts out," Chip said. "But you've got to stay in the book. You knew McStew better than anyone."

"I hardly knew him at all," I said and walked away.

I ran into Corky Perkins, who gave me some tips, before we had to go to class, on how to slide to third base. We used a garbage can for the base.

"Try sliding in head-first," Corky suggested.

"Are you crazy? I could knock myself out."

"Might help your game," he said.

Just then I saw something I couldn't believe. Lynette Stoddard was standing between the jungle gym and the swings, waving to me. At first I thought she meant someone else, but when I pointed to my chest, she nodded. I walked toward her, slowly.

"Hi, Scotty."

All at once my tongue was the size of a meat loaf. Lynette swayed anxiously from foot to foot. Then Corky came over to spoil things. "Hey, Hansen! You want me to teach you to play baseball or what?" he said in a loud voice while gawking at Lynette.

"I already know how to play baseball," I answered, just as loud.

Then Lynette said, "Could I be your first?"

"Yes!" Corky answered. "Yes!" But Lynette ignored him.

"First what?" I asked.

She said, "Everybody says you and McStew were close."

"We were like brothers," I told her.

"Then if it's okay, I'd like to be the first one up in the tree house on Saturday. Chip said it'd be open for us kids."

"I'll make sure you're first," I promised.

"Great! Well—see you Saturday, then." Lynette showed me a crooked little smile that wrapped itself around my heart.

Corky whistled as she walked away. "Forget third base. You're still trying to make it to first!"

The bell rang and we went inside. I didn't hear a word our teacher, Miss Twilley, said all day. All I heard was Lynette's voice, over and over, like the words of a song—"Could I be your first? Could I be your first?" And I could already see us sitting in the tree house, holding hands, like in that picture of Mom and Dad when they were kids.

At lunchtime I said to Chip, "After school today we'd better start getting the tree house ready for Saturday."

"I thought you said to forget it."

"Forget such a terrific idea? Never!"

I should've known that Chip already had everything worked out. "Don't beg people to come," he said. "Let them beg us. Wait until they're ready to pay the highest price, then lay the goods on the table. That's my dad's motto."

For the rest of the week we spread fantastic stories about McStew. Chip even told how McStew once broke into his house and stole his mother's diamond earrings and bought hamburgers for 150 starving kids.

"What if your mom comes to school and hears that story?" I asked.

"Are you kidding? She's too busy getting her hair dyed. She never comes here."

We let as many people as possible know that the tree house would be open for business from 11 a.m. until 2:30 p.m. on Saturday. Mom's shift at the diner lasted from ten until three.

"We'll charge fifteen cents. No, a quarter," said Chip. "If business is good, double that on Sunday."

"Mom doesn't work Sundays."

"Okay, Monday."

After Lynette came and went, I didn't care who came.

By 10:30 Saturday morning there were sixteen kids lined up in our back yard, with more on the way. The idea was for Chip to collect their quarters at the bottom of the ladder. Then I'd give my McStew speech in the tree house—two kids at a time. We'd made a big cardboard sign with the letters "Home of the Gypsy Bandit" written in black crayon.

I told Chip before we got started, "Let Lynette Stoddard come up first and let her come alone. And don't charge her."

"Who says?"

"I say! It's my tree house, remember?"

"I can see you have a lot to learn about business," complained Chip.

I'd stayed awake most of the night thinking what to say to her. I even practiced in front of the mirror when Mom wasn't around, but nothing sounded right. Most of it was corny. What I finally came up with was the truth: "Lynette, I've loved you since second grade and I hope you love me, too." Now, if I could only get her mind off McStew. Wasn't that why she was coming? Wasn't that why they were *all* coming—to hear about McStew?

While kids lined up, I was in the tree house peeping over the edge. They were standing around, shoving, laughing, and talking. Below me, her hand on the rope ladder, was Lynette Stoddard. I felt the same weak feeling I always felt when I saw her. And suddenly I wanted to jump out of the tree and go hide in a bush, but her blond hair was on its way up.

"Oh, hi," I said, as if seeing her was a big surprise.

Lynette looked around. "So this is it, huh? The famous McStew hideout."

"It's not much, really." I wished I had something to do with my hands.

"What's that space over there for?" she asked.

"That? That's the pantry."

"Pantry?" She laughed. "In a tree house?"

"My dad's idea. He drew up the plan. But anyway, I guess you want to hear about—you know. The Gypsy Bandit."

"Listen," said Lynette, turning serious. "I don't want to seem rude, but I don't care about that stuff."

"You don't?"

"No. It's silly. I came here to give you something." She pulled an envelope with my name on it out of her back pocket. "Go ahead, open it—no, wait. Read it after I leave." And I saw her cheeks flush.

We both stood staring at the envelope and I tried to see through it, like Superman.

Finally she said, "Who's F and J?" She pointed to a spot on the oak's trunk.

"My folks. Dad put that there when they were kids."

Lynette smiled and ran her finger over the carved heart. Seeing her do that made me love her all the more.

"Hey, up there!" Chip shouted. "Quit playing house and give someone else a chance!"

Lynette looked embarrassed. "I guess I better go."

"You don't have to."

"But I better." She started down the ladder. "Scotty?" Her blue eyes gazed up at me. "I thought about you all summer."

I nearly fell out of the tree.

Other kids were on their way up. I wanted them to disappear so I could read Lynette's letter in peace. For the time being, I just stuck it inside my shirt.

Stanley Lambertino and Jace Ellis were standing in front of me, but I couldn't think of a single thing to say. My heart was too busy going, "Lynette, Lynette, Lynette." Four kids later, Chip's angry head popped up.

"What's the idea? Everyone says you won't talk. You just stand there grinning at them."

I grinned at Chip.

"Snap out of it, Scotty! Do your job!"

After that, I told a different story to every kid who came up. Stinky Wellman got to hear how McStew was really the son of cutthroat pirates. And Mary French's mouth dropped open when she heard that McStew stayed in the tree house so no one would see the terrible burns he got rescuing babies from a flaming orphanage. The Franklin twins' eyes bugged out when I told them how McStew ate the guts of dead cats and dogs just to stay alive. The Franklin twins were in third grade.

Pretty soon Chip's head popped up again. "Whatever you're doing, keep it up—they love it!"

Every time I opened my mouth, the tales got wilder. I even started acting some of them out, leaping and jumping around the tree house like I was McStew himself. One little girl left with tears in her eyes, and Chip told me not to overdo it.

"His real parents were bank robbers, see, and he stole thousands from them while they slept, then gave it to bums out on the street."

"Bullshit," said Corky Perkins.

"Well, it's true."

"In your dreams." On his way down the ladder Corky said, "Learn how to slide, Hansen!" Then he made Chip give him his quarter back.

"We're in the dough," Chip said when everyone was gone. "There'll be even more kids here on Monday when word gets around." He went into a little dance. "Well, hey, I guess you want your forty percent, huh? After all, it was my idea, right?"

I gave him my mother's look.

"Just joking," he said.

After we divvied up the profits and Chip went home, I settled down in a corner of the tree house to read Lynette's letter. Except it was gone! I nearly tore my shirt apart looking for it. It must've fallen out when I was leaping. But I couldn't find it on the floor, or even on the ground below. Where else could it have gone?

Idiot! How could I lose the most precious thing in my life? I went in the house to call Chip, even though I knew he wouldn't be home yet. My mother was just coming in the front door.

"My poor, sad, aching feet," she moaned. "Can you hear them? They're singing the blues."

I said, "Want a glass of water?"

"Please—one for each foot."

She was stretched out on the couch, wiggling her toes when I got back.

"If it weren't for the tips," Mom said between gulps of water, "I'd quit, but for a diner they're incredible. One man left me five dollars. Then he asked me out."

"You're kidding."

"I'm *not* kidding. Hey, what happened to your shirt? It's torn."

"Huh? Oh. Um . . ."

Mom lifted her head. "Scotty, have you been fighting?"

"No. I just all of a sudden outgrew this."

I went and put my money in my sock drawer, changed into another shirt, then called Chip on the upstairs phone. His mother answered. She could never remember who I was and always sounded as if she was in a bad mood.

"Don't mind her," said Chip a few seconds later. "She doesn't appreciate living with a genius. Hey, I'm glad you called. How does *Tree House of the August Moon* sound? Or do you want to stick with *The Gypsy Bandit*?"

"What?"

"I just figured a new way to get people to pay more money. We'll tell them Hollywood's making a movie about McStew's life."

"Forget about McStew. Did you find an envelope in the yard with my name on it?"

"I kind of like *Tree House of the August Moon*. Even though he built it in June."

"Chip, will you listen! Did you find an envelope, or didn't you?"

"No."

I hung up. I pounded my head with my fist. Idiot!

Some stupid kid must've walked off with the love letter Lynette Stoddard wrote me and maybe was reading it out loud that very moment, with others sitting around listening. What if it was Corky Perkins? Corky was a good ball player, but he had a mean streak as wide as center field.

I searched the yard again, then sat down on the back porch steps, replaying her words in my head: "I thought about you all summer."

Inside, the phone rang and I heard Mom's tired voice answer. I thought, please let it be some extremely kind, wonderful person saying they'd found the envelope and wanted to return it, unopened. But what I heard was my mother's voice telling them goodbye, followed by, "Francis Scott Hansen—come in here!"

When Mom called me Scott Hansen I knew I was in trouble, but when she called me by all three names I knew I was dead. I took my time getting there.

"Yes, Mom?"

"That was Betsy Franklin. Did you tell her twins that McStew ate dead cats?"

"Well, um. I might have," I answered. There was no use lying. She always knew.

Mom's eyes grew wide. "And did you charge them a quarter apiece to hear such nonsense?"

"Er—"

Suddenly her feet didn't ache anymore. They started across the room toward me, but I was saved by the bell. "Hello!" she shouted into the phone.

"That was Pauline Taggart's mother," Mom said after hanging up. "She claims you told Pauline that McStew was an escaped maniac who killed people and buried their body parts in the back yard." She paused. "Well?"

I looked down at the floor.

"Scotty, what on earth—? How many kids did you say these things to?"

I shrugged.

She said, "Well, if the phone rings again, I'm not answering it. It's too embarrassing, and I'm too tired. I just don't know what's gotten into you."

"I'll scrub the kitchen floor if you like."

"What's the kitchen floor have to do with anything?"

I knew that was a job she hated.

"No," said Mom in a quiet voice I hated worse than her loud one, "I'll tell you what you're going to do. You're going to round up whatever money you took from those children—every quarter—and deliver it to each of their houses with hand-written apologies. Do you understand?"

"Chip has half the money," I said.

"Chip? Oh, I might have known. Was this his idea? No, don't even answer that. You're old enough to think for yourself. Now get busy and write those apologies. I won't have people thinking I've raised a hooligan." Her hand was on the phone. "What's Chip's number?" As I started up the stairs I heard her say, "Oh, he most certainly did! Don't let him play innocent with you, Mrs. Keller."

When I got to my room, I sat down with pencil and paper. What came out was not an apology but, "Dear Lynette. I thought about you all summer, too. And last summer, and the summer before that. I've loved you since second grade. Your friend, Scott Hansen."

Then I wrote my apologies.

"Let me see," Mom said when I came down with the notes and a sock full of coins. I had my note to Lynette folded in an envelope in my back pocket. "Well, you've got quite a journey in front of you," said Mom after she inspected my work. "You'd better get going."

I pedaled my bike down the street to the Steinbergs' house. Mrs. Steinberg and her daughter, Lydia, a fourth-grader, were standing on the porch.

"You're basically a sweet boy," said Mrs. Steinberg, "but you have what is known as an overactive imagination. You should perhaps write novels."

Most parents were understanding, although I had to listen while a couple of them gave lectures. They all thanked me for the apologies and asked how Mom and I were getting along.

I hadn't gone far before I ran into Chip Keller, who was pedaling around delivering his own apologies.

"Way to go," he grumbled. "There goes our Hollywood movie."

"It's not *my* fault people called my mother. And anyway, whose bright idea was this?"

"I'm the first Keller in my family's history who's ever had to give money *back*," he complained. "Do you know how humiliating that is?"

I said, "Listen. We can't both go to the same houses. I've already been to the Steinbergs, the Fosters, the Eggmonts, the Bassingtons, and the Miltraps. Right now we're about in the middle, so why don't you take everything north of here and I'll go that way."

Chip nodded. "We've got to do the right thing," he agreed. "And giving the money back is not the right thing—Scotty, I've got a new plan."

"Tell somebody who cares," I said and rode off.

When I got to Lynette Stoddard's block, the grips on

my handlebars turned sweaty. At least I didn't have to write *her* folks an apology. I leaned my bike against a tree across the street, then crept into the Stoddards' yard and crouched behind a bush. I pulled out the envelope and made sure it was sealed tight. The words PERSONAL, PRIVATE, AND CONFIDENTIAL were written in big letters above Lynette's name. When I was sure no one was looking, I tiptoed over to the mailbox and slipped the envelope in. Then I hurried back to my bike and raced off down the street to the Daytons'. I pictured Lynette opening the envelope, reading my words, her eyes filling with tears of joy. I was still grinning when Mrs. Dayton answered the door.

I saved the Franklin house for last, hoping Mrs. Franklin would be in a better mood.

She wasn't.

"My Judy and Jody are *still* shaking!" She got right down in my face. "I'll likely have to take them to a psychiatrist."

"I'm real sorry, Mrs. Franklin."

"Eating dead cat guts. The idea!"

"And dog guts!" one of the twins hollered from inside the house.

"And dog guts," repeated their mother as she read my apology. "As if this is supposed to help. Hmmph!" She went on for several more minutes while I nodded my head and repeated how sorry I was. "Well, I should hope you are," said Mrs. Franklin. "Do you enjoy scaring little girls?"

"No, ma'am," I answered.

"Yes he does!" hollered the voice inside.

I gave Mrs. Franklin two quarters and told her I had to go.

"Wait," she said, and I thought she was going to start in on me again, but she waved a crumpled envelope in my face. "I found this in the pocket of Jody's dress. Lucky for you, I didn't throw it away."

It was Lynette's love letter! I snatched it out of Mrs. Franklin's hands.

"Well, how rude!"

"I'm sorry, Mrs. Franklin, it's just that—"

"Go!" She shooed me out the door, which slammed at my back.

I sat down on the Franklins' stoop and ripped the envelope open. It was a card. On the front was a picture of fat yellow flowers and fancy writing: "Thinking of you." Inside the card was more fancy writing: "In your moment of sorrow may God's grace lighten your load." Below that, in not so fancy writing, were these words, in ink: "So very sorry you lost your dad. Your classmate, Lynette Stoddard."

A freezing wind blew out of the card into my bloodstream, making me numb. Not a love letter at all. A sympathy card!

For a minute, all I could do was sit there. Then I jumped up and banged on the Franklins' door.

"Now what?"

"Mrs. Franklin, can I use your phone? I need to call my mom. It's important."

She frowned and pointed. "By the stairs."

I picked up the phone directory and looked up "Stoddard."

"Don't you know your own number?" asked Mrs. Franklin.

"It's a tough one," I said.

"But you've lived there all your life."

One of the twins was standing by the phone. "My mother says you're bad." She curled her tongue at me through a space between her teeth.

I dialed the Stoddards' number and let it ring and ring and ring. All I wanted was to beg Lynette to please not read my letter. I wasn't sure what reason I'd give— maybe that I had to fix the spelling. Anything to keep her from reading it.

After the thirteenth or fourteenth ring, I hung up. I butted my forehead against the wall. Lynette didn't love me, Lynette didn't love me.

"Oh, now," said Mrs. Franklin. I felt her hand on my arm. "It can't be *that* bad. If I was too hard on you, well, I apologize. Just don't do that to your head. Or my wall."

The twin wagged her finger in my face. I felt like giving it a twist.

But wait—if no one was home at Stoddards', didn't that mean the envelope was still in the mailbox?

I dashed out of the Franklins' house and flew my bike to Lynette's block and parked it across the street like before. There was still no car in the driveway. The coast was clear.

I snuck across like last time, stooped down behind the same bush, then, when I was sure no one was looking, tiptoed up to the mailbox. My hand had just touched its tin lid when a voice behind me said, "What are you doing?"

I dropped down on my hands and knees and started patting the ground.

"I lost my cuff link," I said.

"Cuff link? You're wearing a T-shirt," said Lynette.

"It was my favorite one, too. It had my initials."

"You're weird."

"Just go on with what you were doing. I'll be gone before you know it." All I could see were her shoes, caked with mud.

"Did you, um, read my card?" Lynette asked.

"Yeah," I said. "I read it." I stood up.

"I felt so bad when your—you know, when your dad—I couldn't think of what to say. My mom told me to send a card. I bought one, only I held on to it all summer, don't ask me why. I've never known anyone whose—well, I just didn't want to think about it."

She rattled on like Mrs. Franklin. I just heard half of what she said. All I wanted was to snatch the envelope out of the mailbox and be gone—but not with her standing there.

"So, anyway, I tried a couple of times to give it to you on the playground or in the cafeteria," Lynette explained, "but there were always kids around. I could've mailed it, but I promised myself it had to be in person. And that's why I brought it to the tree house. My folks think I gave it to you last May, back when—" For a minute we stood staring past each other. Then she said, "Scotty, I'm real sorry about your dad."

"Yeah. Me, too." I couldn't think of what else to say, so I said, "Nice shoes."

"I was weeding the flower bed when you crept by," said Lynette.

"I wasn't creeping."

"It sure looked that way."

"It's 'cause I didn't want to wake anyone," I told her.

"But it's five in the afternoon." Lynette folded her arms. "Just what are you up to, anyway?"

"Me? Nothing. I came over to thank you for the card."

She unfolded her arms. "I'm sorry it took all summer."

"That's all right."

"Well, I guess you better go. If I find your cuff link I'll bring it to school," said Lynette, smiling her crooked smile, and I forced myself down the walk. I was almost to the curb when she said, "Scott Hansen?" I turned and saw her take a piece of paper from her pocket. "All summer's a long time not to tell somebody something. But second grade? That seems like forever."

Just then her parents' car came down the street and Lynette hurried inside.

My bike carried me home over rooftops and through clouds of glory—she'd held my letter against her heart.

The Perfect
Scarecrow

"Okay, so tell me."

"Tell you what?"

"You know."

"Silly. I already told you." She was squatting on Mc-Stew's blanket in a corner of the tree house and I kept rubbing my eyes to make sure she was really there. I'd imagined it so many times. It was a Saturday afternoon in late October. The weather had turned cool, and the neighborhood smelled of burning leaves. One street over, I could hear kids shouting and tossing a football around, but I was happy to sit in my tree house with Lynette Stoddard. "I've had a crush on you, too," she practically whispered.

"Yeah? How long?" I grinned from ear to ear.

"Since"—one eye squinted shut like she was counting the years—"last Saturday."

"Last Saturday?"

"The minute I read your letter—it was so romantic."

"But I've had a crush on you since second grade."

"I know. And that's what's so romantic."

"But it doesn't seem equal."

"Aren't you glad I have a crush on you at all?" Lynette asked.

What I wanted then was to sit by her and hold her hand. I wanted it more than anything, even more than playing for the Yankees. But we'd only been dating since noon, so I decided to stay where I was.

"This tree house is so neat," Lynette said. "I can't believe you guys built it yourselves."

"I just did the roof and painted it. McStew did the rest."

"McStew?"

"It doesn't even leak."

"Do you think he was crazy?"

"I put on a ton of tar paper, which is why."

"People say he was."

"My mom says McStew was a victim of his parents," I told her. "His dad beat him."

"McStew had a dad?"

"Well, he never came home much. When he did, it got pretty rough. Sometimes we'd hear him throwing things. Mom called the cops but nothing happened. And McStew's mom—well—" I pretended I was drinking a glass of whiskey.

Lynette shivered and hugged her knees.

"Cold?" I hoped she'd ask me to come over and put my arm around her.

"Do you know oaks are the last trees to lose their

leaves in the fall? My daddy says so. He's a pharmacist."

"Your dad owns a farm?" I said, just for laughs.

"I feel so sorry for him."

"Why? The farm isn't doing well?"

"McStew. I feel sorry for McStew. What you just said. I was trying to change the subject so I wouldn't think about it, but it keeps coming back."

"Oh, don't worry about McStew," I said. "He lives in a castle, surrounded by a thousand servants."

"Now, don't start that up again." Lynette frowned, and she looked so pretty sitting there with her chin resting on her knees, her hair the color of butterscotch pudding, that I wished I could keep her in the tree house forever. That's how good she looked. I also wished she would look up at the place on the trunk where my parents' "F & J" was carved. Because right beneath it, in a freshly carved heart, were the letters "S & L." I kept glancing up there, hoping she would, too.

"Do you ever hear from him?" Lynette asked.

"Hear from who?"

"Whom."

"What?"

"McStew."

"No."

"I wonder where he is, what he's doing?"

"You know those stories Chip and I made up? He could be doing any one of them."

"He's probably rotting away in an orphanage somewhere," said Lynette.

"McStew? Nah. Not him."

Cool air blew leaves into the tree house and one clung to her hair like a decoration. She said, "So why did his dad beat him?"

"I thought you didn't care about that stuff."

"I don't care about that Gypsy Bandit routine you and Chip cooked up."

I said, "He used to beat McStew's mom, too. Sometimes we'd see them with cuts and bruises."

Lynette shivered again, not from the cold, and hugged her knees even tighter. "Daddy never even spanked me when I was little," she said. "He just looked real hurt over things I did and that was enough to make me stop." She smiled. "Know what I miss most about being a little kid?"

I shrugged.

"Riding around on his shoulders. I remember going through streets on days like this. I liked reaching up and touching the leaves. Once I banged my forehead on a branch and got this nasty welt? It was the only time I saw Daddy cry." She said, "Scotty, did you ever ride on your dad's shoulders?"

"Oh, sure—every day."

"There were other things, too. Sometimes he'd cover the living-room furniture with all the bedspreads and blankets in the house so we'd have this enormous tent? Then I'd get my dolls and we'd sit under it, just Daddy and me, eating snacks and sipping cocoa. Like we were camping. And he'd read me stories."

Except for *The Swiss Family Robinson*, which he read during the last weeks of his life, I don't remember my dad reading anything except work reports. There were times, though, back when I was little, Dad made up stories about this funny little guy called the Fudge Monkey, who was always causing mischief. I got the idea (I'm not sure how) that the Fudge Monkey was Dad himself when he was little, and the stories he told weren't totally made up. They weren't bad, either; I looked forward to them. But as I got older, the Fudge Monkey stories stopped coming. I could barely remember them.

"So, anyway, that's why I feel sorry for McStew," said Lynette. "I mean, gosh—his dad and all." Then she looked embarrassed. "Want to go for a walk?"

"Sure—why not?"

We started down the rope ladder, when suddenly Toby poked his gray face through the hedge that separated our yard from the Stewarts'.

"Oh, look, a cat," said Lynette.

"You want him?"

"Why? Is he a stray?"

"He belongs to my mom."

"Silly. You can't give away your mother's cat."

Ever since McStew got hauled away by cops, Toby spent most of his time in the Stewarts' back yard. I'd see him prowling around, and sometimes he'd make weird noises in the night.

"How old is he, anyway?" Lynette asked.

"He was my great-grandfather's cat when he was a boy," I said.

"You're kidding!"

"So I guess that would make him around a hundred and forty."

Lynette slapped my arm. "I knew you were kidding!"

Toby ducked back into the hedge.

"So why don't you like him?" Lynette asked.

"He steals my baseball cards."

"A *cat*?"

"Then buries them in McStew's yard."

"Why's he do that?"

"Ask him. Let me know what he says."

"A cat who steals baseball cards. Now I've heard everything."

I got down first and held the ladder. Her sleeve brushed my cheek and I could smell laundry soap.

Just then Mom stepped outside the porch door. She had on her favorite blue sweater, the one she wore on cool days after she got home from work.

"Hello, Scotty."

"Hi, Mom."

"Lynette, honey, aren't you chilly?"

"No, I'm fine, Mrs. Hansen," said Lynette, and I saw her teeth chatter.

"Scotty, I thought you were going to rake up the leaves around front."

"We were just going for a walk," I said.

"I can help," Lynette volunteered.

"The rake and wheelbarrow are in the garage," said Mom, and Lynette raced around the side of the house to get them.

"So"—Mom smiled, folding her arms—"is it burning leaves I smell or is romance in the air?"

"We're friends," I whispered, even though Lynette was not there to hear.

"Yes, I can see that." In practically the same breath she added, "I'm starting a new job."

"What? You're quitting Mac's Diner?" There went my free milk shakes.

"Remember the man I told you about who comes in and leaves five-dollar tips?"

"The guy who asked you out?"

"Oh, that was just a tease," Mom said, blushing. "Anyway, he owns a business downtown and wants me to come work for him. I'll make a salary plus commission."

"What do you mean—a tease?" I asked.

"It's Ragland Shoes. You know. Where your father bought his loafers."

I made a face. "You're going to sell *shoes*?"

"We'll get discounts."

"I'd rather get milk shakes."

Just then Lynette came back with the wheelbarrow. She said, "How about if you rake and I load. Then we'll switch."

"And afterwards everyone come in for cider," said Mom, and she went inside.

"So, Scotty, what're you going to be for Halloween?" Lynette asked as we went around front.

"Nothing. I'm too old."

"Me, too. This'll be the first Halloween I get to stay in and hand out treats. Do you know Daddy took me around trick-or-treating clear up until last year? I think he was afraid I'd get kidnapped."

"Did you ride on his shoulders?"

"Silly."

I watched Lynette pick up leaves, and for about the millionth time I pictured the two of us cuddled up in the tree house, the world drifting by like October leaves.

As she bent to scoop up an armful, I took off my jacket and laid it across her shoulders.

"Hey."

"Your teeth were chattering," I said.

"When you called to invite me, I hurried off without my sweater."

"It's the best call I ever made," I said, and felt my heart beat like a tom-tom. It'd taken me all morning to make that call. I'd even rehearsed it in the mirror, holding a shoe up to my ear: "Lynette. Hi. It's me. Scott Hansen? I was wondering—" When I finally picked up the phone and dialed for real, she said before I even finished asking, "Sure, Scotty, I'd love to! I'll be right over!" And here she was.

Lynette put her hands on my shoulders and brought her face close to mine. I could feel her breath. "Know what I'm going to do for you?"

"W-what?" I asked and got my lips ready.

"Help you with your math."

"My what?"

"I've seen how you struggle with fractions."

"Sure. Great. And I'll help you with English."

"Oh, you don't have to. I make all A's."

We heard a car horn. I turned to see a brand-new '59 white Buick with blue writing and a phone number on the door back up from in front of McStew's house. The driver leaned over the passenger seat and rolled down the window. A cigarette dangled from his lips. "You kids live here?"

"I do," I said.

"How'd ya like to make a buck?"

I started walking over but Lynette grabbed my arm. "Don't. He could be a kidnapper."

"Kidnappers don't write their phone numbers on their cars," I said.

"Thing is," said the man from inside a cloud of smoke, "that yard needs rakin' bad and we're shorta help—innerested?"

I glanced at McStew's front yard. It was a blanket of leaves.

"How much?"

"A buck." The man nodded at Lynette. "The both yas."

"Make it four," I said. "Four apiece."

"Four? Jesus, kid, we're talkin' leaves, not rocks."

"I'm using my own rake and wheelbarrow," I pointed out.

The man took a drag off his cigarette. "I'll go two. Two's my offer. An' yous pick up every last leaf."

"We'll take the money now." I held out my hand.

The man reached inside his coat. I thought, if only Chip could see me. Of course, without Lynette watching, I never would've talked that brave. "Here's two," he grunted. "Two more when the job's done."

After he drove off, I figured Lynette would be proud of me, but she said, "That man could've kidnapped you."

"The company he works for owns this house. It said so on his car."

"Even so."

I handed her the two bills. "I'll take the next two."

We pushed the wheelbarrow into the middle of Mc-Stew's yard, then took turns raking and picking up just like we'd done in mine. Not only was I in love, I was making money. Life was good.

Pretty soon Mom came out. "What on earth?"

"We got a better offer." I told her about the man in the Buick. "But don't worry. We'll finish our yard when we're done here."

"Well, I guess there's something to be said for earning a little extra cash." Mom looked thoughtful. "And who knows? Maybe we'll get neighbors who behave themselves." She brought us each a cup of cider, then went back to the house.

Lynette took her turn with the rake. She said, "Look what I found." She held up a rusty cap pistol.

"If you think *that's* something, wait'll you see what's buried around back," I told her.

In a while a brown station wagon eased up to the curb and the driver gave three quick honks.

"Daddy!" Lynette dropped the rake and sped toward the car. Remembering something, she stopped, spun around, and handed me my jacket along with her smile.

"Will you come back tomorrow?" I asked.

"Sure. Right after church, if they'll let me."

For a split second I thought she'd kiss me. Instead, she raced over to the station wagon and kissed her father. For I don't know how long after they left, I stood leaning on the rake, daydreaming. The next thing I knew, the guy in the Buick was back.

"Hey, kid," he called to me from his window, "you 'spectin' them leaves to rake themselves?"

I said, "I'm nearly done with the front. Okay if we do the rest tomorrow? There're no trees out back. All the leaves blew over from neighbors' yards. It won't take long."

"Keep in mind I got prospects comin' Monday," said the man. "We want this place lookin' tip-top." And the car sped off down the street.

When Mom called me for dinner, I was still leaning on my rake, breathing in the smell of laundry soap from my jacket.

The next morning I got up early, showered, combed my hair, doused myself with cologne, and put on my best clothes.

Mom looked me over at the breakfast table. "Who precisely are you, sir, and what have you done with my son?"

"Huh? Oh—I just felt like getting a little dressed up. You know."

"A little?" She straightened my tie. "So I guess this means Lynette's coming over."

"Who? Oh—I don't know. I've got leaves to rake."

"In your Sunday clothes?"

I shrugged and took a look at the clock. Mom waved her hand in front of her face. "Goodness. Is that your father's cologne I smell?"

I said, "I hope you don't mind. I found it in the medicine cabinet."

"I don't mind, but I can't guarantee what the rest of the neighborhood will think," said Mom, still waving her hand.

"It's that strong?"

"Put it this way. If Frank had worn that much when we first married, you wouldn't be here."

"Huh?"

"Such a young man—oh, my goodness!"

"What?"

"Well, I—I guess this means we're going to have to have a little talk."

"What little talk?"

"You know—a little talk." I saw her blush. "About—well—things. But we don't have to do that today. To-day's Sunday, so not today." She refilled her coffee cup and hurried out of the room, as if someone had just called her name. I was pretty sure she meant the same little talk Corky Perkins gave me back in the fourth grade—only without certain words.

After sticking my face under the bathroom faucet for several minutes, I went around to McStew's back yard and waited for church to be over. Everything looked dead: the yard, the bushes, the house itself. No one had lived there since summer. In September, cleaning crews showed up with ladders and buckets of paint, but to me the place still looked dead.

I wondered who in their right mind was thinking about moving in. I'd never once set foot inside. McStew never invited me—I guess because of his crazy parents.

Kids in the neighborhood liked to pretend the Stew-art house was haunted, and that McStew came from a family of pirates who hid their victims under the floor-boards, which was why the place stank so bad. Chip and I had made up so many stories that nobody knew what to believe. And then there was Toby howling in the mid-dle of the night.

"What ails that cat?" Mom would ask.

"I think he misses McStew," I'd answer.

I stood on tiptoe with my hands cupped against a windowpane, when the sound of crunching leaves made me turn.

"What's wrong? Did you see a ghost?" asked Lynette.

"Just shadows," I answered, glad it was her.

"Don't you look nice. Were you in church?"

I shook my head. The last time I was in church was when Dad died.

"So are you ready to rake leaves?" I asked. I noticed she was still wearing *her* Sunday clothes, and together we looked like the top of somebody's wedding cake.

Lynette reached into the folds of her dress and pulled out the two dollars I'd given her. She said, "Daddy says I can't do this. He says this whole McStew thing is out of line."

"But McStew's not here."

"It's not just that. He and Mom heard about that stunt you and Chip pulled, and"—she hung her head—"he says you're a bad influence."

"But didn't you have fun yesterday?"

"Scotty, I'm sorry. I have to go."

I felt my heart sink. "Maybe if I go talk to him. Maybe if he sees how wonderful I look—"

"You don't get it. I've never had a boyfriend."

"So? Neither have I. I mean—"

Just then Toby raced past. He had something in his mouth.

"Look—there goes another baseball card," said Lynette.

"He can have them all, if only you'll stay."

She surprised me by hiking up her dress and charging after Toby. I charged after Lynette.

The dirt was loose and lumpy in the corner of the yard where Toby dug. When he saw us, he dropped the card and ran up a tree. Lynette picked the card up—a Joe DiMaggio—and handed it to me. Then she pointed at something on the ground. "Somebody's shoe."

"Tell your dad I hardly knew McStew," I said.

"Who would bury a shoe?"

"Tell him I can't even remember what McStew looks like."

She leaned over to pick up the shoe but it was stuck in the dirt.

"S-Scotty," she said.

"Tell him that deep down I'm a fine human being."

Lynette's eyes were suddenly the size of kneecaps and her face turned chalky white. She was trying to say something but no words came out. Then I saw that the shoe had a foot in it. The foot was attached to a leg. Everything else was covered with dirt.

Lynette put her hands over her mouth and made gagging sounds. Then she turned and ran out of the yard like she'd been set on fire. I stared at the foot. The shoe no longer fit it. Lying next to the foot was McStew's cowboy hat, ruined by rain.

I didn't hear him, not until he spoke: "So whadja do, scare off your lady friend? And how come these leaves aren't— Holy Mother of God!" The man who drove the white Buick dropped his cigarette and dug his fingers into my shoulder. "Tell me that thing's not real! Tell me it's a Halloween prank!"

I pushed him away and bolted for the hedge, tripped,

and smacked my forehead against something on the ground. I tried to get up but fell face-first in the dirt. That's all I remember.

When I opened my eyes again, I was flat on my back in bed staring up at old Doc Vance. My mother was holding my hand.

"—every couple of hours or so," the doctor was saying, "and remember to check that compress. Also—well, well, look who's joined us." His false teeth smiled at me.

"Scotty!" Mom said, squeezing my hand. "Can you speak?"

"What's your name, son?" asked Doc Vance. His face reminded me of chewed gum.

"Who won the World Series?" asked Mom.

"McStew," I groaned.

"He thinks he's McStew." The doctor frowned.

"He—he's buried out back," I said.

"Thank God!" Mom kissed my cheek.

"But McStew—"

"Scotty, that wasn't McStew." Mom spoke through tears. "The police identified the body. It was McStew's father." She and the doctor exchanged glances. "Now rest. You have a bump."

I slept the rest of the day. When I woke up again, Doc Vance was gone and the room was filled with shadows. Mom sat by my bed holding an ice pack.

"Did Lynette call?" was the first thing out of my mouth.

"Are you thirsty?" Mom asked. I nodded and she gave me water. "No—she didn't."

I closed my eyes. Everything hurt. Especially my heart.

"What happened?"

"You tripped over Toby and hit your head on a skil-let," Mom said.

"I meant McStew's father. What happened?"

She shook her head and pressed her lips together.

"Mom?"

"What is it, son?"

"I had a dream."

"Oh?"

"It was about Dad. He wasn't dead. We were in the tree house together. He was—we were reading a book. There was all the time in the world. Nobody had to be anywhere."

"That sounds like a wonderful dream." She squeezed my hand.

"Mom?"

"I'm right here. I won't leave. I won't ever leave."

Her hand felt clammy.

I slept.

For the next few days the neighborhood swarmed with cops. They searched McStew's house and yard, looking for clues. As soon as Mom let them, they had a ton of questions for me. At first I was afraid they thought *I* killed Mr. Stewart, especially when the man in the black suit showed up—the man I called the Warden. I hated the way he looked at me.

"You mean to say you never smelled anything?"

"We thought it was the rabbit."

"The rabbit."

"Mrs. Stewart had a rabbit."

"Which you were supposed to rescue," Mom re-minded me.

"We already have a cat," I said.

"Let's get back on the subject," said the Warden. The way he had of staring at me after I answered his questions reminded me of a teacher. He'd taken out a little notebook and pencil. "So when was the last time you saw Mr. Jeremy Stewart?"

"I only saw his leg."

"Alive."

"I don't remember."

Mom spoke up. "I'm afraid we heard him more than we saw him. He wasn't a very nice man, you know. He hurt his family."

"Was he stabbed or shot?" I wanted to know, but the Warden never answered anybody else's questions, just asked his own.

"The son—Mick Stewart. Did he ever speak to you about his father?"

"He never talked about his family," I said. "He mostly hung out with Reese."

The man wrote "Reese" down in his notebook. "Where can I find this Reese?" he asked.

"He could be anywhere."

Right about then Toby passed by, and I thought, that's the guy they should be grilling. He knows everything.

Pretty soon I got bored answering the same stupid things over and over, and Mom came to my rescue by shooing the cops away.

They also asked the guy who drove the Buick a bunch of stuff. Once I looked out and saw him knocking his head against a tree in McStew's front yard. He'd lost a sale, but I'd lost the love of my life. Also, I had a knot on my forehead the size of a gum ball. Combing my hair forward didn't help.

I was miserable. Even staying home from school didn't help. All I could think about was Lynette, Mc-Stew, and McStew's dad—but mostly Lynette. I'd go to the phone, stare at it for a while, then walk away. I thought if only I could talk to her, get her up in the tree house—if only.

Mom put her arm around me. "Nothing I can say will erase your pain. However, the key is to keep busy. That I learned from experience." She said, "Something else you need to know. Mr. Stoddard called. He forbids you to see his daughter until—what did he say? Until she's fifty. Foolish man. He needs to get over himself."

I went up to my room and buried my head in the blankets. Life was over. To make matters worse, the man from the diner who gave Mom big tips and got her to come work for him—the Shoe Guy, I called him— kept coming over, trying to be buddy-buddy, squeezing my arm and acting like he was my dad or something. Mom got so she called him whenever the cops wanted to question me, as if his being there would make a differ-ence. I wanted them *all* to go away.

Then on Wednesday afternoon, while I sat on the couch feeling sorry for myself, the doorbell rang. I took my time answering it, pretending Lynette would be there smiling her crooked smile. But it was Chip Keller.

"Miss Twilley sent you a present—here." He jammed a pile of homework in my arms.

"Jeez, what can she be thinking?" I said. "I'll be back tomorrow."

"Forget homework," said Chip, breezing past me into the room. "What I have to say will change your life."

I said, "Go away."

"Don't you know you're living next door to a gold mine? McStew's dad was *murdered*. Bashed in the skull with a 'blunt instrument.' Do you know what that means?"

"It means our street's turning into a carnival. People keep driving by just to get a look. My mom says if it keeps up we might have to move."

Chip slapped his forehead. "Do I have to explain everything? Now I know how teachers must feel. What it *means* is, we can charge people to come into that house next door and see the very room where McStew's mom did the murder."

"How do you know it was McStew's mom, and how do you know where she did it, even if it was her?"

Chip said, "Oh, brother. When you hit your head, some brains must've leaked out. I know she did it because she confessed!"

"No fooling?"

"And we can *make up* the place where she did it—let's say the kitchen, because she probably used a rolling pin."

"McStew's mom a murderer—wow." I had a picture of Mrs. Stewart in her black-and-blue checkered dress sneaking up behind Mr. Stewart with the rolling pin in one hand and the rabbit in the other.

"Yeah, it's pretty tragic, all right," said Chip, "but, hey—we'll make a fortune."

"You're crazy. That place is locked up tight. And anyway, it belongs to some guy in a white car. He'd never let you in."

"Moron! We sneak in at night. That's when it's the spookiest and kids'll pay big bucks. Plus, tomorrow's Halloween. Oh, man, what timing!" Chip went into his little dance. "Scotty, an opportunity like this doesn't come around every day. By Thanksgiving it'll be too late."

I tried changing the subject. "How're the kids at school? Glenn, Sam, Pete? Lynette?"

"At least think it over."

"Do they miss me? Corky, Ross, Donny? *Lynette?*"

"Corky says he can't wait for you to get back," said Chip. "He wants to hear all about the dead body you saw. You're the only kid in school who's seen a murdered dead guy. That's how I know we'll make a fortune."

I opened the front door and shoved him out.

"Wait. You haven't heard the best part yet!"

I closed the door.

An hour or so later Mom came home from her new job, all smiles. "I love it, love it, love it!" She twinkletoed around the room like she was in a Hollywood musical. "The people are so nice and friendly. Can you believe it? Not a grouch in the bunch."

"A week from now you'll be complaining," I said.

"Oh, quit being negative. I will not."

"Your feet'll hurt like they always do."

"Speaking of feet—guess what? We get free shoes."

"I told you, I'd rather get free milk shakes."

"Shoes are expensive," Mom said. "Look." She

reached into a box and pulled out what looked like two heavy brown logs—wing-tips. "These are for you."

I jumped back. "You don't think I'm going to wear *those*."

"They're patent leather. Very stylish. And see? Mr. Ragland had your name and phone number stitched on the insides."

"And that's supposed to make me like them?"

Mom gave me her look and I knew it was time to change the subject. "Chip said McStew's mom confessed to the murder."

She nodded and a pained look spread over her face. "It was on yesterday's news. They found her—the police, I mean—in some seedy hotel downtown. She admitted to it right off the bat."

"Well, if you knew yesterday, why didn't you tell me?"

"Oh, I don't know—you've had such a hard week, I didn't want to add to it. Then, too"—Mom tried to put her hands on my shoulders, but I backed away—"you're still my little boy and I want to protect you from—well—things." She threw her hands up. "I know, I know, you're twelve. But, Scotty, let's face it, it's been a tough year. Losing your father—"

"My father. I can tell you're thinking about him."

"What's that supposed to mean?"

"These." I picked up the wing-tips and dropped them on the floor. The whole house shook. "And him." I pointed at the box with "Ragland" printed on it.

I watched Mom's body stiffen. She folded her arms and said, "Well, since you're so grownup all of a sudden,

I suppose you can handle this. Your friend ran away."

"Ran away? From where?"

"He was in a foster home. When the police went to question him, he was gone."

"McStew? In a foster home?"

"Well, certainly. Where else would he be? On a pirate ship or one of those other ridiculous places you and Chip dreamed up? We're talking about a child's life here."

"McStew's McStew," I said, not knowing what I meant.

"If that boy were here right now, I'd give him a hug," said Mom. "He's been through so much."

"What about all *I've* been through? My father's dead, too."

"His father beat him."

"Mine never paid attention. Isn't that as bad?"

She unfolded her arms. "It's always about you, isn't it?" Mom said, heading for the stairs. "Your misfortunes, your sad life. Well, maybe one day you'll take a look around and see there are others who are worse off." She paused. "Mrs. Stewart admitted to killing her husband, all right. But who do you think buried him in the back yard?"

I pictured McStew's cowboy hat lying in the dirt by the leg sticking out of the ground.

"So in case you think this is some kind of kid's game," Mom continued, "keep in mind that that boy is scared senseless, wherever he is. Remember those bruises? It's quite possible that his mother was protecting him from that—that *low-life* she married. And

McStew, in turn, was protecting her by hiding the body." She shook her head. "And you think you have problems." She went up the stairs.

I slumped down on the couch and pressed a finger against the bump on my brow. Everything was awful. Lynette didn't love me. Mom was working for the Shoe Guy. McStew's dad was dead. *My* dad was dead. Mc-Stew had run away—

So dammit, I *did* have problems.

I hated everybody: Lynette's dad, my mom, the Shoe Guy, Miss Twilley for sending homework, Chip for bringing it, Toby the cat, the Warden, the guy in the white Buick—everybody. I felt like chewing a hole through the couch. Instead, I grabbed those cruddy shoes off the floor and ran out back. I didn't have the guts to throw them away, but I didn't mind hiding them in the tree house. It was something the Fudge Monkey might do. I sat up there until Mom called me for dinner.

We ate in silence. I wouldn't look at her and I doubt that she looked at me. The first time she spoke was later, when the phone rang. She straight-armed it out to me.

It was Chip.

"Know what would've been an act of genius?" Chip said. "If when you found that body you'd hid it under some leaves—"

"Chip—"

"Then we could've propped it on a stick in the back yard and kids would've paid their allowances to see the perfect scarecrow."

"That's sick."

"That's business. But don't sweat it. We'll still make a bundle. Here's how."

I slammed the phone down.

"Well, *that* was rude," said my mother. "I hope you're not that rude on Friday. I invited Cliff to dinner."

"Who?"

"Mr. Ragland—my boss."

"Aw, jeez, anyone but him."

"Don't start."

"Just tell him not to squeeze my arm, okay?" I said and went up to my room to listen to the radio. All the sad songs were about me.

Sitting in bed in my pajamas with a comic book propped on my knees, I couldn't help thinking how rotten life was. Finally I leaned over and switched off the light and the radio. The window was open a crack and the room felt chilly. When I got up to close it, a whoosh of cold air slid into my pajamas. And I saw somebody signal to me from a window in McStew's dark and empty house.

McStew
Rides Again

Halloween. But my heart wasn't in it.

Kids at school crowded around me in their stupid costumes (my first day back after hurting my head), all of them wanting to know about McStew's dad, and what it was like to touch a murdered dead guy.

"I never touched him," I said.

"But Lynette did, right? And she was with you."

Lynette. A name that used to make my heart fly into the clouds now made it sink like a stone in a pond.

Corky Perkins grinned while giving me the news: "Her ol' man stuck her in a private school. But here's a naked picture I drew of her right before she left. It's yours. Free of charge."

I sat in class and stared at my desk while Miss Twilley rattled on about the same sorry grammar lesson as before I left. Listening to her was like watching a rerun of the news.

"What do you *mean* you're not going trick-or-treating?" asked Sam Porter, racing around me in his Superman cape at recess.

"I'm too old," I told him.

"Not me, I'll never be too old!" Sam said, and flew across the playground.

"Aha! Just the guy I'm looking for." Chip Keller rushed up to me at lunchtime.

"Get lost," I said.

"I need you to get me into McStew's house tonight."

"Nobody can get in there. It's locked up."

Which was true. The guy in the white Buick had sent some guys over to put padlocks on the doors to keep people like Chip out.

"Oh, I bet you can figure a way." He nudged me.

"I've never been in there in my life," I said, which was also true. I came an inch from telling Chip about the dream I'd had—that I'd seen someone in an upstairs bedroom window—but I bit my tongue. He would've just worked that into his nutty scheme to make money.

But what if it wasn't a dream?

"This is your last chance," Chip said.

"Promise?"

As I walked home through Jollyman Park, I could already hear shouts of "Trick or treat" coming from younger kids whose parents took them around early. I pictured Lynette Stoddard sitting on her father's shoulders in some fairy-princess outfit, smiling and waving at me from far away. Because suddenly that's what she was—a princess in a tower—and there was no way I could get to her.

I kicked through the fallen leaves and remembered a year ago when I raced home, wolfed down my dinner, and leaped into my astronaut costume in time to meet Corky and Ross and some other kids at the park by five-thirty. We split up and covered entire neighborhoods to see who could bring back the most loot. Corky won, as usual, but Ross told me later that he'd done it by scaring little kids into turning their candy over. All that seemed like a century ago.

When I got home, Mom was on the phone (her day off), twisting the cord around her finger and giggling like a schoolgirl.

"Noo. Really?—oh, ha-ha, sure, but—oh, wait, here he is now." She covered the mouthpiece with her hand. "Scotty, didn't I hear you say you weren't going trick-or-treating?"

"Why?" I asked.

She stamped her foot. "Are you or aren't you?"

"Aren't."

"Cliff?" she spoke into the phone. "How does six sound? Great. See you in a couple of hours." She hung up. The smile she had for him was still on her face when she looked at me. "I want you to hand out candy to trick-or-treaters."

"Where are *you* going?"

"I have to step out for a while—business."

"You mean the Shoe Guy," I muttered.

"For your information, I have a job, and unless I get the proper training, I can't do it right."

"Who goes for shoe training on Halloween?" I asked.

"Can you handle being alone for an hour or two, or should I call Mrs. Murton from across the street to come sit with you?" She went into the kitchen to fix an early dinner. I grabbed a handful of candy corn from the plastic pumpkin by the front door and stuffed it into my mouth. Then I plopped down on the couch to read a comic book.

"Now, remember not to hand out great gobs of candy to anyone, or we'll run out," Mom said at dinner. "And don't let anyone in the house. Keep the porch light on. Mrs. Murton's number is by the phone along with the number where you can reach me. Since she's right across the street, you can wave to her now and then to show everything's okay." Mom was going on like Miss Twilley. "You probably won't get many small ones because of what went on next door, but I suspect the older kids will break their necks getting over here." She clucked her tongue. "Isn't it pitiful how someone else's misfortune will bring people out of the woodwork?"

I said, "Why can't we just turn the lights out and pretend no one's home?"

"Oh, and wake up tomorrow with our windows soaped and toilet paper dripping from the trees? I don't think so."

Right before six, Mom came downstairs in her red high-heeled shoes and red lipstick. She wore a red-striped dress and carried a beaded handbag Dad gave her the Christmas before last.

"Oh, *I* get it," I said. "*You're* going trick-or-treating."

"I'll pretend I didn't hear that." She patted her hairdo in the mirror at the foot of the stairs, then reached into her handbag for the car keys. "Now, you know what to do, right? The number's by the phone," she reminded me.

"Jeez, Mom, are you going to be gone for two hours or two weeks?"

The number she left was not the number of her job, so I figured it had to be to the Shoe Guy's house. As soon as she was out the door, I dialed it. Sure enough, the Shoe Guy answered.

"Beware of witches in red shoes!" I said in a deep, growly voice.

"What? Hello? Who is this?"

I quick hung up the phone.

The doorbell rang. "Trick or treat! Trick or treat!"

It was weird, dropping handfuls of candy into other kids' bags. I felt like somebody's father.

"Hey, aren't you Scotty Hansen?" squeaked a little voice from behind a bedsheet.

"No, I'm his twin brother."

"Well, where is he?"

"Next door, hacking up dead bodies."

The sheet sailed off down the walk and tripped over itself, scattering candy over the pavement.

I thought, This might turn out to be a fun night after all.

I sat on the couch and tried to write a letter but couldn't get past "Dear Mr. Stoddard." I hardly knew the man, so how could I convince him that I was a decent human being?

"Dear Mr. Stoddard, I'm a decent human being."

Too braggy. I crumpled it up.

"Dear Mr. Stoddard, I love your daughter and I'm pretty sure she loves me—"

I could picture him hustling over to my house with a shotgun after reading that. So I crumpled it up, too.

"Dear Mr. Stoddard, Are you a Yankees fan? How about I come over and rake your leaves? I promise not to look at your daughter."

Into the trash.

The doorbell rang and the hooded figure of Death stood on the other side of the screen with moths fluttering around his rubber scythe. "Trick," he moaned, "or tre-e-at!"

"We're all out of candy," I said. "Will lima beans be all right?"

Death didn't answer, just stood there moaning. Then he reached out a bony hand and yanked open the screen door. The next thing I knew, he was in the house, clicking off lights. I raced for the phone but couldn't see how to dial. I felt the phone cord twist around my neck and tried yelling for help, but his hand pressed against my mouth. Then I heard Chip's stupid voice.

"You moron!" I pushed him away.

"Gotcha!" He whipped off his black hood, laughing like a hyena. "Admit it, Scotty! I scared you! How wet are your pants?"

"Turn those lights back on before Mrs. Murton calls the cops."

"Excellent costume, huh? Just think how good it'll look next door in the dark."

"I ought to whip your butt."

"Ooh, big talk now that he knows it's me—but listen. I found a way to get into the house."

I switched the lights back on.

Chip said, "A basement window around back is open."

"All the windows are locked. I tried them myself," I said.

"Not this one. Are you coming?"

"Nothing doing."

"Oh, yeah, I forgot—you're a grownup now. Well, at least hand these out." Chip reached into his trick-or-treat bag and pulled out some hand-printed advertisements: "Enter at your own risk. Fifty cents a *head*." "Clever, huh? I got my dumb sister to print them up. So what do you think?"

"This is what I think." I grabbed hold of his black robe and hauled him out of the house.

"Does this mean you don't like the idea?" he called to me from the front yard.

In between trick-or-treaters I would return to the couch with my pen and paper.

"Dear Mr. Stoddard, Seen any good movies lately?"

Ross Hooker and Corky Perkins showed up. Ross was dressed like a baseball player and Corky was dressed like the Devil.

"Take my word for it," said Corky, poking Ross with his pretend pitchfork. "This guy's one hell of a shortstop—get it? One *hell* of a shortstop!" Corky couldn't stop laughing at his own joke. Finally he said, "So what's the deal, Hansen? Why aren't you out here with us?"

"I'm not in the mood," I said.

"Remember when he used to be fun?" Ross elbowed Corky.

"No—when was that?" said Corky, and they howled their heads off.

I said, "If you guys were half as funny as you think you are—"

I watched them go next door and take turns running up onto the Stewarts' shadowy porch, but neither stayed long. Kids had been doing that all evening. Nobody lasted more than a few seconds. Most didn't even make it past the "No Trespassing" sign before chickening out. I remembered my dream from the night before and wondered if Chip had made it inside. Nothing moved. The windows were black and silent.

It *had* to have been a dream.

Mrs. Murton waved to me from across the street. Corky and Ross were trooping up her walk. In the next instant she was shaking her finger and shooing them away. Corky's "hell of a shortstop" joke probably didn't go over that well. Since I didn't have any trick-or-treaters right then, I decided to call up Mrs. Murton. I dialed her number and disguised my voice. "Hello—is Roy there?"

"Excuse me?"

"Roy. Tell him it's important."

"I'm sorry, but there isn't anyone here by that name," said Mrs. Murton.

"Then can I leave a message?"

"You have the wrong—"

"Tell him the next time he wants someone strangled he can do it himself! It's too hard on my fingers, plus I don't know what to do with the body!" I hung up the phone, waited a few seconds, then called back in a different voice. "Hi, this is Roy. Have there been any messages for me?"

I hung up and raced back to the door so Mrs. Murton would think I'd been there all along. I smiled and waved, but she didn't wave back. Just then my own phone rang and I picked it up, half afraid it would be Roy.

"Scotty, did you call up here a while ago?"

"Who's this?"

"You know perfectly well who this is!"

"Oh, hi, Mom."

"Cliff says he got a prank call."

"Well, what's he expect? It's Halloween."

"I'll tell you what *you* can expect when I get home."

I was reaching into the plastic pumpkin for some candy when Chip's face pressed against the screen door. He wasn't wearing his Death hood. Sweat dripped from his face and his cheeks and nose were dirty.

"That's the scariest face I've seen all night," I said.

"Let me in!"

"I believe the magic words are 'Trick or treat.' "

He came in anyway. He was out of breath and his eyes bugged out like candy apples. "That place really *is* haunted. Something touched me—no, grabbed me—I swear it!"

"Yeah, sure."

"I was nosing around upstairs and, and, something whizzed past. Something gray—no, black."

I laughed. "You jerk. That was my mom's cat."

"Whatever it was, it screeched at me."

"Yep, that was Toby, all right. He's weird."

"And that's when somebody, or something, grabbed me. I think it was more like some *thing*."

"Look, Chip, you might scare other kids with that hocus-pocus, but this is me, Scotty, remember?"

Chip grabbed the front of my shirt. "I'm telling you, something got hold of me in the dark and shoved me down." He pointed to his torn pants leg and bloody knee. "See? I barely got out alive!"

"Okay—fine—I believe you."

"You do?"

"Yeah—now go home."

"Okay, but first let me use your bathroom. Then the phone."

I listened while Chip called his mother and begged her to come pick him up. I could hear her yelling clear across the room: "Your legs carried you over there, your legs can carry you back!"

"Put your Death hood on," I told him. "No one'll mess with you then."

"Something's over there," Chip whispered as he walked past me. "Something not human. If I were you, I'd move to another neighborhood. Another *state*." Then he took off running down the sidewalk, bumping into some trick-or-treaters.

I hid the plastic pumpkin behind the door. "Sorry," I told the next batch of kids. "We ran out. Try across the street."

After they went away, I closed the door. I picked up the pumpkin, then went out to the garage to get a flashlight. I crept around side of the house and snuck through the hedge that separated our house from the Stewarts'. Clicking on the flashlight, I sprayed its beam over the back of the house, down low, until I saw the basement window Chip described. Sure enough, it was open. I took a deep breath before going over to the window, which was set down in a little well. A scrap of Chip's black cape hung from a rusty nail.

"McStew," I said, but didn't wait around for an answer. I dropped the plastic pumpkin into the well, then hurried home.

Before long, Mom came in. I was lying on the couch, watching TV. She threw her purse into a chair, turned the TV off, and stood in front of it with her hands on her hips. "Well? What do you have to say for yourself?"

"Why's your lipstick smeared?" I asked, and she covered her mouth with her hand.

"Don't answer my question with a question." Mom spoke through her fingers. "I want to know what you've been up to."

"Handing out candy, like you said."

"Scotty, I know you've been on the phone. Not just with Cliff, but with Mrs. Murton. She flagged me over as I was getting out of the car. Do you really think you're so clever that people can't recognize your voice?"

I didn't know what to say. But Mom knew. She always knew.

"Up to your room. Go!" She pointed as if she thought I'd forgotten the way. I dragged myself off the couch. "Seems I can't leave you alone for a minute. And you can just forget about eating any leftover trick-or-treat candy."

"It's gone," I said.

"What do you mean, gone?"

"There were mobs of kids. We ran out."

"So where's the pumpkin?"

"The pumpkin? Oh. The pumpkin. I, uh, I gave it away—as a door prize."

Mom just stared at me. "Go!" she said.

I sat on the foot of my bed with the lights off and the radio low, staring out at the house next door, hoping for something to happen. I felt positive that Chip would go around yelling his head off to everyone about how someone or something was holed up in the Stewart house, but I felt equally positive no one would listen. Chip was so full of wild stories that kids had stopped believing him.

The house was dark as death, and as quiet. The next thing I knew, the light switched on in my room and Mom was shaking me. I'd fallen asleep in my clothes. Her face was thick with cold cream and bobby pins sprouted out of her head.

"Take me to your leader," I said.

"Very funny. Now, how about getting ready for bed." She stood in the doorway for a minute before going to her room. She said, "I came in here to remind you that Cliff is coming for dinner tomorrow night and unless you want that tree house to become your permanent home, you'd better be on your best behavior." Then she went away.

I slipped out of my clothes and crawled into bed, not even bothering with pajamas. I turned off the lamp and stared long and hard at the upstairs window next door. "Where are you?" I whispered to the darkness. "Why'd you come back?"

Early the next morning, while Mom was taking a

bath, I dashed over to the Stewarts' back yard. The plastic pumpkin was empty.

"Hey, McStew!" I called through the basement window. "Can you hear me?"

After a while I went back to my house and raided the refrigerator for things I didn't think Mom would miss—slices of bread, some grapes, an apple, a banana. I got out the peanut butter and jelly and a knife and was sitting at the kitchen table making sandwiches when Mom shuffled in in her bathrobe.

"What's this?" she asked.

"I woke up starved," I said.

"And you're going to eat all that?"

"I'll take some for lunch."

Mom went to the refrigerator and poured herself some orange juice. "Scotty, I don't want you wasting food. Remember—"

"I know, the orphans."

"Not just the orphans."

"The Chinese."

"And?"

"The Africans." I rattled off other names from a list I'd learned by heart.

"So how about putting most of it back? You can't be that hungry."

"Yes, Mom."

As soon as she went upstairs, I put the stuff in a paper bag and hurried over to McStew's back yard and dropped it into the plastic pumpkin.

That day in class, all I could do was daydream and scribble Lynette's name inside my notebook. I heard

Miss Twilley rap her pointer stick against the blackboard. Her voice called me from a hundred miles away: "Scott Hansen—Scott Hansen?"

"Huh? What?"

"Do you by any chance still attend this school?"

"Yes, ma'am."

"Then please act like it."

The kids around me snickered and I stuck my nose in a book to pretend I cared.

After school I went straight home, and just as I expected, the pumpkin was empty, except for the grapes.

"McStew!" I shouted. "I know you're in there, so answer me!"

Nothing. Complete silence.

I climbed into the tree house to think about what I should do. McStew was wanted by the police for burying his father. But of course his father beat both him and his mother, so who could blame him? On the other hand, it's against the law to bury your father in the back yard. I wondered if I should tell someone, and if so, who? Or "whom," as Lynette would say.

No one came to mind, except for my mom, and she and I weren't getting along too well. So I decided I'd better just keep it to myself, at least for now. I sat down to write a note. When Mom got home, she called to me through the porch door. I folded the note and stuck it in my pocket, then climbed down the rope ladder.

"Now remember, Mr. Ragland is coming for dinner," Mom said.

"How can I forget? You keep reminding me."

"He says it's fine for you to call him Cliff. I just want you to keep your promise about being courteous."

"I never promised," I said.

"You're promising now!" Mom gave me her stare.

"Okay, but tell him not to touch me. I don't like people trying to act like my dad when they're not."

"You lead such a sorrowful life. It's a wonder someone doesn't write a book." She made me follow her into the kitchen. "Here," she said, handing me Crisco and waxed paper. "Go grease the muffin pan."

While I greased the muffin pan, peeled the potatoes, and scrubbed out the coffee pot, I thought about McStew staying in that spooky old house all alone. Just the thought of it gave me the creeps. But something else gave me the creeps even more. What if Chip was right and it was someone or something else, not McStew?

Suddenly I heard Mom's voice. "Are you trying to scrub holes in that coffee pot?"

"Sorry."

"How about setting the table?"

I was arranging plates, silverware, and cloth napkins on the dining-room table when Mom came in with a bouquet of flowers. "Aren't these lovely? I picked them up at the florist on my way home— Say, whose place is that way down at the end?"

"What's-his-name's—the Shoe Guy's."

"Well, if he sits that far away, he might as well eat downtown."

"Good idea." I snatched the plate up.

"Scotty." Mom pointed to where she wanted it.

"But that was Dad's place," I said.

"All right, then. Over here—by you."

I plopped the plate down with a clatter.

"Well, I can see *this* isn't going to work," Mom said.

"Him and his stupid shoe jokes. Not only that, he's bald."

"What's that got to do with anything? He's a nice man."

"So? Your other bosses were nice. You didn't invite *them* for dinner."

"This may come as a big surprise to you, but I need friends, too, and Mr. Ragland—" She turned red in the face. "Just set the table. He'll be here at six. And call him by his name, will you, and not the Shoe Guy."

Sure enough, the Shoe Guy rang our bell right at six. I answered the door while Mom fled upstairs to make sure she looked right.

"Well, hi there, Scott! How's the head?" The Shoe Guy spoke in a loud voice. He held a bouquet of flowers just like the ones on the table.

"We already have flowers," I told him.

"Mind if I come in?"

I nudged the screen door open with the toe of my shoe and he stepped inside.

"My oh my, something sure smells good."

"Mom broiled steaks."

"Steak, my favorite!" He squeezed my arm.

Just then Mom came sailing down the stairs in her red lipstick. "Why, Cliff, don't you look smart."

"And you, Marie—you look radiant." He handed her the flowers and she acted like she'd never seen anything quite like them. Then they stood there gazing at each other. It was embarrassing.

"Scott says we're having steak," said the Shoe Guy.

"Steak? We're having Swedish meatballs. He knows that."

"Swedish meatballs, my favorite!" said the Shoe Guy.

"Maybe if she got a raise we could have steak," I said.

Mom shoved the flowers in my face. "Put these in water, you."

While I was in the kitchen filling up a vase, Mom blew in like a hurricane. "One more crack like that and those flowers will go on your grave. Do you understand?"

"I was trying to make conversation."

"Well, do it with your mouth shut."

Supper was a bore. It was like sitting in Miss Twilley's class, except, instead of hearing about fractions, state capitals, and nouns and verbs, I had to hear about fallen arches, support lifts, and ingrown toenails. The Shoe Guy rambled on like it was the most fascinating stuff on earth. I thought my face would fall in my mashed potatoes, but Mom sat with her chin propped on her hand, clinging to every word. I looked around at our plates. I'd barely touched mine and Mom didn't seem to know there was food in front of her. I felt like reminding her about those Chinese and Africans. But the Shoe Guy shoveled his down like he hadn't eaten since Tuesday. Words flew out and food flew in. Soon his plate was as shiny as his head. He dragged a napkin across his chin and finished telling another stupid shoe joke.

"So I said, 'That loafer had better hold its tongue!' " Then he laughed so hard he shook. Mom threw her head back and laughed, too, even though there wasn't one thing funny.

"Oh, Cliff," Mom said, "you card, you!" Then she

said, "Please help yourself to seconds while I go fill
the gravy boat." She touched him on the sleeve.

"Seems I do have room for a tad more at that." The
Shoe Guy patted his stomach and reached for the
mashed potatoes—as if he needed any. While Mom was
in the kitchen, the room got quiet.

"So, Scott. I understand you're quite the Yankees
fan," the Shoe Guy said.

"They're okay."

"Okay? They're the best we've got. But what kind of
season are they going to have?"

"How can anyone know? This is only November."

"Oh, right—well, hey. Here's wishing them all the
best." He raised his water glass. He didn't know the
first thing about baseball. We both stared at the door to
the kitchen like we couldn't wait for the gravy boat to
get back. Then the Shoe Guy, his mouth chomping
salad, said, "How the shoes fit?"

"Shoes?"

"Your mother gave me your foot size, but if they're
the least bit uncomfortable—"

"Oh, those."

"And what did you think about your name and phone
number on the insides?"

I shrugged. "Okay, I guess. It's just that, who loses
their shoes?"

"Truth is, Scott, it's in case you were to, say, get lost
or something. Your shoes would identify you."

"Oh, you mean in case I got murdered, they'd know
who I was."

"That's not what I—"

Mom breezed in. "Gravy, everyone!"

"May I be excused?"

"Scotty, you've hardly eaten a bite."

"Neither have you."

"Excused!"

I was about to remove my plate when Mom said, "How about making yourself useful and put on some music before you go. Something soothing—the London Philharmonic would be nice. Is that all right with you, Cliff?"

I could tell by the look on his face that "Pop! Goes the Weasel" would've been all right if my mother had suggested it.

While Mom and the Shoe Guy talked, I went over to the record cabinet and fingered through my parents' albums, which no one played anymore. And I had a sudden flash. I slipped a disc out of its sleeve and put it on the turntable, lowered the needle, then grabbed my plate and made for the kitchen. Behind me I heard Frank Sinatra singing what Mom and Dad used to call "their song," the one that always made her cry.

With the plate of food still in my hand, I went straight out the back door and through the hedge. I crept over to the basement window and set the plate down next to the empty pumpkin. Then I took the note out of my pocket that I'd written earlier: "McStew. If you want me to keep bringing stuff I will but let me know it's you okay? Durango."

I dropped the note into the pumpkin and headed back to the house, glancing over my shoulder. I thought I saw a light or a candle in an upstairs window, but it was only the reflection of a street lamp.

I decided it was better to go around front. That way I

could sneak upstairs without talking to Mom or the Shoe Guy. My teeth chattered because I didn't have on my jacket, or I'd have sat in the tree house for a while. When I got around the corner of the house, I was surprised to see the Shoe Guy get into his car and drive off.

Inside, Mom still sat at the dining-room table while the Frank Sinatra record played. From where I stood, I could see the second helping of mashed potatoes on the Shoe Guy's plate. I was about to go upstairs but something made me walk over to the table instead. Mom had her head bent over her plate like she was praying.

"Mom?"

"Why'd you do it?" She lifted her face and her eyes were wet. "Why?" She wasn't yelling and she didn't act angry, she was just asking me something I couldn't answer. "I guess it's because you don't think I deserve any happiness," she said. "I guess you think I should be a mother and a widow and nothing else. Well, let me tell you." Her voice was very low and un-Mom-like. "I loved your father, and there's not a day goes by I don't think about him in some way or another, even if it's only for a minute or two. But—" Her eyes were on the record player, on Frank Sinatra. She got up from the table. "You're not the only one around here he didn't pay enough attention to." And she started gathering things off the table, dirty dishes, uneaten food.

"I can do that," I offered.

"No." She spoke in the same low voice. "What you did tonight was embarrassing and inexcusable. So why don't you just go off and do whatever it is you do. Because right now, Scotty—right now I don't like you very much." She went into the kitchen and I went up to my room. I grabbed my jacket and rushed outside onto the dark sidewalk, searching up and down the chilly street, thinking if I could just find the Shoe Guy, if I could get him to come back and finish his mashed potatoes and tell another shoe joke, things would be fine. But the street was empty.

I went around back to climb the oak tree. Even at night, the tree house always made me feel better, no matter what the problem was. Only this time I felt like my brain wanted to explode, so much was crammed inside it—Mom, the Shoe Guy, Lynette, McStew—just a big jumble of awful feelings.

When I got to the top of the rope ladder, something leaped past me to the ground below, nearly making me fall. It was Toby.

"Guess he still doesn't like you," said a voice inside the house.

"McStew!"

He reached out his hand to pull me up. I felt like I was face-to-face with a ghost. He looked taller, older, almost unreal.

"Why're you here?" I asked.

"Broke out of the slammer," he answered. "Too bad I had to shoot some guards." He looked around. "Nice roof."

"How'd you get here?"

"I came to get some favors," said McStew. He pulled a wrinkled envelope out of his pocket. "See that Blackheart's wench gets this."

"Your mom? Where is she?"

"Sheriff's got her in the hoosegow, or I'd deliver it myself."

The envelope was sealed. I could tell it had a card inside.

"Stole it from a general store," McStew explained. "Reese stood lookout."

"How'd you know I'd be here?"

"I've waited these past few nights. I figured you'd show up sooner or later. Daylight's too risky—posse's on my trail."

"Yeah, I heard."

"I got two more favors," said McStew. "First, don't tell anyone you saw me." He looked around as if the tree house were surrounded by sheriff's deputies and his horse stood saddled and waiting beneath the branches.

"Where will you go?" I asked. "Who will you stay with?"

"Out west, where I belong. I'll stay where I like."

I imagined windswept prairies with setting suns and snow-capped mountains, saloons with swinging doors and dusty streets.

I said, "Can I go?"

"Someone's got to stay here and mind the ranch," McStew answered. It sounded like the same kind of lame excuse my dad used to give when he didn't want me tagging along. "Here." He held out his hand and gave me what looked like a pointed stone.

"What's this?" I said.

"Slug from a .44. My lucky bullet. I dug it out of Reese's chest right before he died."

"Reese is dead?"

"Ambushed. Caught in a crossfire."

"I thought you said this bullet was lucky."

"For me, not Reese. He blocked it—saved my life."

I couldn't have been more surprised than if Reese had been real.

McStew said, "Keep it—so you won't forget me."

As if I could ever forget McStew.

"Next to Reese," he said, "you're my best friend. And now that he's gone—" There in the dark, I could almost swear he was crying, but of course he wasn't. He was McStew.

I said, "So what's the other favor?"

"Take care of my cat."

"What, Toby?"

"He's a decent animal and great company on a chilly night. Don't put him in any more washing machines and maybe he'll like you better."

"That's a tough one," I said.

"The card—not to tell anyone—and Toby. I want you to swear on this bullet."

"I swear," I said, squeezing McStew's lucky bullet. McStew squeezed my hand.

"Well," he said, "time to ride."

"At this hour?"

"Less chance of getting caught." He picked up the plastic pumpkin, which I didn't notice until then. "Thanks for the grub. I'll eat it along the way."

"I can get some more," I told him.

"This'll do fine." He smiled and put his hand on my shoulder. "Durango."

The light in our bathroom suddenly switched on and

I could see his face real plain. There were no tears. Working up my nerve, I said, "I was wondering something. Were you there when—I mean—when she hit him with the rolling pin?"

McStew narrowed his eyes at his empty house. "It wasn't a rolling pin," he said. "It was a gin bottle." The bathroom light clicked back off and we were in the dark again. "And it wasn't her that hit him."

"Then who—"

"She was on the floor, bleeding. Blackheart had just punched her in the mouth." McStew kept staring at the house, as if he were watching the whole thing over again. "It ached my hands, it hit so hard. I brought it down with all my might. It didn't break like you'd have thought. Ma was proud of that. I could barely drag him across the yard, even with Reese's help."

"You mean *you*—?"

"He had it coming," said McStew, then pointed his finger at me like a six-gun. "Just remember your promise." He started toward the ladder. I noticed he had on the old vest he sometimes wore and some scuffed-up cowboy boots.

"McStew, wait." I grabbed the shoes I'd hidden up there, the ones from the Shoe Guy, and handed them to him.

He turned them over in his hands a couple of times. "These? These are dude shoes," he said.

"You might need a disguise. And if you're going to walk out west, an extra pair will come in handy."

"Haven't you heard of stagecoaches?"

"Call me when you get there. My phone number's inside the shoes."

For once it was McStew's turn to look surprised. "Calling's risky. People listen."

"Then change your voice. Make up a secret code. Like, 'Don't forget the green paint.' " I tried to crack a smile. "Or something."

McStew bundled the shoes inside a cloth bag. Then he was gone, leaving me with the card to his mother and the "bullet" that killed Reese.

How long I stayed in the tree I don't know, but when I looked over at the house, all the lights were out and it was as dark as the Stewart house. Mom must've gone to bed, thinking I was already asleep. Angry as she was, maybe she hadn't bothered to peek in on me like she usually did. Or maybe she just didn't care.

I knew the doors would be locked, so I climbed the tree by the kitchen and eased my way across the slanted roof over the porch to my bedroom window, which was unlatched. For quite a while I just stood in my room with the lights out, thinking faster than what my brain could handle.

Finally I tiptoed down the hall to Mom's room. As usual, her door was open a crack. I stepped inside, real quiet, hoping she'd be awake.

"Mom?"

I could hear her breathing. It was the breathing of sleep. I stood by her bed. The book she'd been reading lay on the floor. She was curled up under the covers like a little kid, one arm stretched across the space where Dad used to be.

I don't know what made me do it, but I knelt down and picked up a lock of her hair and rubbed it between my fingers. "Mom," I whispered, "I'm sorry." She went on sleeping. Quiet as a cat, I took off my shoes and jacket and crawled under the covers at the bottom of her bed. Sometime during the night her foot kicked me in the ear, and I woke up just as the Gypsy Bandit and I were shouting and shooting our way into the badlands of New Mexico.

Your
Gypsy Smile

"So when're we going to California?" I asked.

"Who said anything about California?" Mom answered.

"You did. You said that's where you wanted to go."

"Oh, that was ages ago. Your father promised to take me."

"Dad's gone," I pointed out.

"Yes, I believe I know that."

"So does that mean *we* can't go?"

"Push the can in closer," said Mom, meaning the trash can. It was Saturday morning and we were sitting at the kitchen table, peeling potatoes. She was making all kinds of things for Thanksgiving, which was the following week.

"I mean, when people die, does that mean people who are still alive can't go to California?"

"Scotty, you're wearing me out with your gibberish."

"Look at McStew. His father died and *he* went west."

"How do you know?"

"How? Well—I don't. But that's where he always said he'd go."

"Oh, I see, and now you want to go because you think you might see McStew along the way, is that it?" Mom shook her head. "That poor boy. It's a wonder no one's found him by now. I just hope—" She reached for a potato.

"You hope what?"

"That nothing's happened."

"Like what?"

"Like anything."

"What could happen? He's McStew."

Mom let out a long breath and leaned forward in her chair. "Scotty, take a look outside. Do you see how cold it is? McStew's a twelve-year-old boy, like you. Not an ordinary boy, I grant you, but still flesh and blood with the same vulnerabilities as anyone else. Who do you think's going to feed him, clothe him, give him shelter? My God, if it was you I'd be scared senseless."

I stared at the frosted windowpanes. Snow covered everything. It covered the roof of the tree house.

"What's wrong?" she asked.

"Nothing."

For a while the only sound was the ticking of the radiator. The kitchen was very warm. Then Mom said, "When McStew ran away from that foster home, he probably just kept going. On the other hand, if he were to get in touch with someone, who do you suppose it would be?" Her eyes met mine.

"I haven't seen him," I said.

"I'm sure you haven't, or you would have said something."

"I think I'll go outside." I got up to wash my hands.

"Don't forget your earmuffs," said Mom. "And if you think of anything else you want to tell me, you know where I am." She went on peeling potatoes.

I'd made a promise, I kept telling myself as I put on my coat. In fact, I'd made three promises. It had been more than a couple of weeks since I mailed McStew's card to his mother in the city jail, and I hadn't let on to a single soul that I'd seen him in the tree house.

As I pulled on my boots, Toby bunched himself into a ball and stared at me from under a chair. "Here, kitty," I said. "Here, kitty, kitty." I held out my hand in friendship, but he looked at it like it might be hiding a weapon.

The really big secret, though, the biggest secret of all, was the one I'd never tell—that it was McStew who killed his father, not McStew's mother, like everyone thought. If they caught him, he'd go to the electric chair.

On my way out the door, another thought slammed into my brain. If the police never learned the truth, then McStew's mother would go to the electric chair for something she didn't do. She was innocent, and no one knew but me.

Suddenly I felt sick to my stomach. There was no way out. One way or another, somebody was going to the electric chair, and no matter who it was, it would be my fault.

I went out back. For some reason, sitting in the tree

house always made me think better, and I sure had a lot to think about. Huddled up like an Indian chief, I pretended my breath was smoke signals. I made believe I was high up on some snow-covered mountain, a hermit who never saw anyone or talked to anyone or made promises.

Scattered on the floor around me were unfinished letters I'd written to Lynette Stoddard:

"Dear Lynette, I miss you—"

"Dear Lynette, School isn't the same without you. Neither am I. You said you'd help me with fractions. Maybe one day we could get together and—"

"Dear Lynette, Tell your dad it's not my fault I have crazy neighbors who kill their relatives and bury them in the back yard—"

I wadded the letters into a fat ball and pitched it into a corner. Beneath the carved heart with my parents' "F & J" was the heart I'd carved into the trunk with the letters "S & L." I tried rubbing them out but they were in too deep.

Outside, the snow came down in chunks the size of golf balls. My ears began to sting, but I wouldn't leave the tree house until I had a plan that would keep McStew *and* his mother out of the electric chair. If my ears fell off in the meantime, then that was the price I'd pay.

But all at once the plan popped into my head like an answer on a math quiz. It was perfect!

What I'd do, I'd wait until just before Mrs. Stewart, with chains dragging from her wrists and ankles, was to walk down that long, lonely hall to the electric chair.

I knew what it looked like because of the movies. I'd call up the jail and tell them everything I knew, that McStew was the real killer, not her, and she would go free just in the nick of time. By then McStew would be so far away no one would find him. And if the police wanted to stick *me* in a jail cell for not telling sooner—well, fine. Anything for a friend.

But in order for my plan to work I needed to know when Mrs. Stewart was going to the electric chair. That meant I had to give up at least part of McStew's secret. And I would need my mother's help.

I climbed down the rope ladder and went through the porch into the steamy kitchen. There was Mom rolling dough for piecrust. Cans, jars, dishes, bowls, pie tins, and cookie cutters were scattered over the table and counters. Everything looked almost as powdery white inside the house as out.

"Why are you making so much food?" I asked.

"I thought I told you to wear earmuffs."

"I forgot."

"I'm fixing Thanksgiving dinner. We're having guests. Hand me that flour sifter."

"Yeah, but how *many* guests?"

"I don't know yet. I only know that this is our first Thanksgiving without Frank and we're not about to spend it alone—even if I have to invite in the whole neighborhood."

I said, "Are you thinking about inviting *him*? The Sh—I mean—Mr. Ragland?"

"Under the circumstances," said Mom without looking up, "I hardly think it's appropriate."

"It's all right with me if you do," I said.

"Oh, isn't that generous of you!" Mom slammed her fist into the pie dough. "I'm sorry, Scotty," she said. "I didn't mean to snap your head off. My decision has nothing to do with you."

"But I thought you liked him."

"I did. I do. But it's just too soon. I was lonely, is all, and—I'm over that now." She pounded the dough again. "Who knows? Maybe I'll invite Miss Twilley and your teacher from last year. Mrs. Mackley."

"You wouldn't!"

"I might. We can eat cranberry sauce and discuss adverbs."

"Aw, jeez," I said. I couldn't imagine anything worse.

But at least Mom had her sense of humor back. For a couple of days after I played the Sinatra record, making her cry and driving the Shoe Guy out of the house, she quit speaking to me. She also quit her job at Ragland Shoes and quit answering the phone. Long-stemmed roses showed up every few days, delivered by the same chilly-looking guy with buck teeth and chapped lips.

"Roses in November," Mom muttered to herself. "Must cost him a fortune." She didn't open the little envelopes the cards came in, but she did keep the roses. Our house started looking like a funeral parlor.

Tired of being ignored, I sat down and wrote her an apology with all the words spelled right and in my neatest handwriting. I signed my full name—Francis Scott Hansen—at the bottom of the paper. After she finished reading it, she didn't say a word, just rushed over and gave me a hug that went on too long. "Okay, Mom, okay." I said. But at least we were buddies again.

"He's a dear, sweet man," Mom said once, her finger on a rose petal. "I told him the day I left my job that I couldn't see him again. He'll have to accept that." But her finger had lingered on the rose.

Now, while Mom cracked eggs into a bowl, I worked up my courage to say, "I sent her a card."

"You sent who a card?"

"Whom. Mrs. Stewart. I sent it to her in jail."

"Oh?"

"Yeah. In case she—you know—goes to the you-know-what."

Mom was busy reading a recipe and wasn't paying attention.

I said, "I mean, people who murder people, that's where they go, right?"

"Scotty, what are you rattling on about?"

"Mrs. Stewart. Do you think she'll get the electric chair for what she did?"

"I'm sure I have no idea," said Mom, brushing flour off the tip of her nose. "That's for a judge and jury to decide."

"But you'll let me know if it happens, won't you? I mean, in case I miss the news that day."

Mom stopped what she was doing. "What kind of card did you send?"

"A get-well card."

"A get-well card?"

"To show I was thinking about her."

"Since when are you so concerned about Mrs. Stewart?"

I shrugged.

"Now, let me get this straight," said Mom. "You're

telling me that you, Francis Scott Hansen, actually took it upon yourself to go to a store, pick out a card, pay for it with your own money, sign it, stamp it, and then you sent it to Mrs. Stewart in jail. Is that right?"

"Right."

"And what did you write on it?"

"Write?"

"The card—what did you write?"

" 'Better luck in the future.' "

"All right, now suppose you tell me what's really going on here."

"What do you mean?"

"Scotty, do you think after all these years I can't tell when you're up to something? Out with it. What's on your mind? I have work to do."

"The card was from McStew, not me." Those words slipped out before I could stop them.

"McStew? So you did see him. Where? And when?" Mom asked. She set aside her flour sifter.

Without meaning to, I'd broken my promise and I knew she would see through any lie I told from that moment on. I said, "In the tree house. A couple of weeks ago."

"And you didn't tell me?"

"I promised McStew. He gave me a card to give to his mom and—" I was beginning to feel scared.

I could see by the way her bottom lip was sucked in that Mom was trying to decide what to do. Suddenly I felt like Mrs. Stewart, waiting for the judge and jury. But all Mom did was lay her floury hands on my shoulders.

"Keeping a promise is an honorable thing," she said. "But sometimes it's more honorable to break one. You'll have to learn the difference. Did McStew say where he was going?"

"West."

"Where west?"

"Just west," I said. And I told her about the shoes.

She wiped her hands on her apron and went straight to the phone. I stood by and listened to her repeat to the cops everything I'd just told her. When she hung up, I said, "Are they coming to arrest me?"

"No, but they'll want to ask you some questions— what he said, what he was wearing, things like that."

"I never thought anything bad would happen," I said, hating the whiny sound my voice made. My eyes were fixed on the frozen tree house outside the window.

"And probably nothing will. But, Scotty, what you must understand is, he's without parents, without a home, and all anyone wants is to bring him to safety."

And all *I'd* wanted was to keep McStew out of the electric chair. What was his crime? He'd killed a man who was hurting his mom and him. He didn't deserve to die and neither did she. But now he could be lying at the bottom of an icy river on account of me not telling.

"Now, listen," said Mom, once again tuning in on my thoughts. "There's not much else you can do right now. If you don't keep your mind occupied, you'll make yourself sick. For starters, how about checking the mail? Then come back and I'll give you some chores."

On my way out the door, I promised myself I'd never do anything wrong again. From now on, I'd think only good thoughts and do good deeds. Forever and ever.

But I broke that promise as soon as I got to the mailbox. The mailman hadn't come yet, but inside was a folded-up rose-colored piece of paper with Mom's name on it. Taking it out, I saw "Ragland Shoes" printed at the top and a letter to Mom in blue ink with "Cliff" signed at the bottom. Without giving it a thought, I slipped the paper into my coat pocket and hurried back to the tree house. I climbed inside, settled myself down, and read the Shoe Guy's letter to my mother:

> *Dearest Marie,*
>   *How many times have I started this?*
> *Ten? Twenty? A hundred? Maybe this*
> *time I'll actually finish, but no words seem*
> *to suffice. I want you to know how fully I*
> *accept your decision not to see me. It was*
> *way too soon. I should have realized that*
> *from the start. But should your heart ever*
> *mend to the point that a friend is needed*
> *and roses are possible, I will feel honored*
> *to answer the call.*
>   *I miss your gypsy smile.*
>
>   *Cliff*

I laid the letter down and barely had time to think about it when a blue knit cap poked up through the opening of the tree house, along with red cheeks and a runny nose—the Shoe Guy!

"Mind if I come in?" he asked, and was already

swinging one leg up. "How about if I take that." He aimed a gloved finger at the letter, which I handed over at once. "Where I come from, stealing mail's a federal offense."

"I—I'm sorry." I couldn't believe he was in the tree house. He was old—in his thirties—like my mom.

The Shoe Guy squatted down. "You don't think much of me, do you?" he said. "I run a shoe store. That's not exciting like being a cowboy or a ballplayer. But it still doesn't entitle you to steal my mail."

"I said I was sorry." It crossed my mind that he might be some psycho killer with a knife under his coat.

He glanced at the letter, then stuck it inside his pocket. "But who knows?" He sighed. "Maybe you did me a service."

"What do you mean?"

"I'd have only embarrassed myself if she actually read this."

"How did you know I even had it?" I asked, and he looked sheepish.

"I watched you from across the street."

"You mean you were spying?"

"Watching, not spying."

"Same thing."

The Shoe Guy reached into his coat and I thought, uh-oh, here comes the knife, but all he did was pull out a handkerchief and blow his nose. "Call it what you like. To tell the truth, I was hoping for a glimpse of your mother. What I got was you stealing my letter."

"I was going to put it back," I said.

"Of course you were." He blew his nose again. "Something you don't seem to realize, Scott—your mother is a very special lady. She's one of a kind."

"One of her's enough."

"Well, naturally, you and I have two different viewpoints. But I'll let you in on something. I used to go to Mac's Diner just to watch her wait on customers."

"You're kidding."

"The food isn't that great."

"Oh, but those milk shakes," I said. "I got to eat free until she went to work for *you*."

"Life is full of misery," said the Shoe Guy. "So what do you want—an apology?" He patted the pocket with the letter inside. "I think I've spilled my heart out enough for one day."

"I thought only kids did stuff like that—sneaking around, spying on girls."

"Here's a news flash for you, my friend," said the Shoe Guy. "You never outgrow stuff like that. No matter how old you are or what you do with your life, there will always be some girl's smile to keep you awake at night. If you're lucky."

I glanced at the wadded-up ball of letters to Lynette Stoddard in one cold corner of the tree house.

The Shoe Guy pulled himself to his feet and so did I.

"Well, I'll be going along now," he said, then looked worried. "I just hope she didn't see me."

"Are you going to tell?" I asked.

"How about this? You don't tell and I don't tell."

"Deal."

He stamped his feet and flapped his arms. "Man, is it ever cold up here. When are you going to put in central heating?"

"There's some things my dad didn't think of," I said, and the Shoe Guy's face sagged.

"Now, that's a ghost I'll never get past."

"Huh?"

"I mean no disrespect, but—" He squeezed my arm. "Listen, Scott. Just for the record—nobody can ever replace your dad, not me or anybody else. It was never my intention to try, and since we won't be seeing each other again, I just thought I'd better say it."

"All right."

Then he said, "I know from experience how hard it is to lose someone."

"Why? Did your dad die?"

"There are more ways to lose somebody than through death," said the Shoe Guy.

As we stood there in the tree house with snow floating down around us, his hand on my arm suddenly felt like a hug. I pulled away.

"Well," he said, and started down the ladder.

I don't know what made me do it, but I said, "You could walk in and hand it to her, you know."

"Excuse me?"

"Your letter. She's in the kitchen making stuff for Thanksgiving. You could walk in and hand it to her."

"What, and get my head broken?"

I said, "She gets loud and she gets angry. She even gets weird. But she never gets mean."

He stared up at me for a long moment, his nose running like crazy. The blue cap pulled over one ear made him look goofy, like one of those boxers who's been hit too many times—not handsome like those pictures of Dad, and not like anyone I'd dream my mom would want to kiss. But I never dreamed she had a "gypsy smile," either—whatever that was.

"What have you got to lose?" I said.

"Wish me luck," said the Shoe Guy.

I watched him go down the ladder and make tracks through the snow to our back door. Before giving myself a chance to change my mind, I scrambled out of the tree house and plodded off to the garage, where I rooted out the snow shovel Dad gave me for my birthday two years before. Other kids got train sets and catcher's mitts. I got a snow shovel.

"To earn yourself some money. To become self-sufficient," Dad had explained. "Someday you'll be grateful you have it." I remember thinking that that day would be a long way off.

I headed down the street with the shovel slung over my shoulder as if I were a soldier marching off to war. The snowflakes were bullets that couldn't harm me. I didn't stop until I was in front of the Stoddards' house.

I started at the bottom of the walk, scooping as much snow onto my shovel as I could, then heaving it onto the lawn. There had been snow for three days straight and it was still coming. I pretended that I was saving the universe and had to make it all the way to the Stoddards' front door, or else the earth, stars, moon, sun, everything, would blow up. I kept on shoveling, not worrying whether anyone was watching or not. With every shovelful I made believe I'd saved someone from destruction: "This one's for Lynette—this one's for Mom—this one's for McStew—this is for the Shoe Guy—here's for Dad—for both grandpas and grandmas—" I counted dead people, too, since if the whole universe blew up, it could interfere with them, wherever they were. "Here's for John Wayne—this is for Elvis—Aunt Sue's new baby—Aunt Sue and Uncle Don—Chip—Ross—Corky—McStew's mom—the Yankees—"

The Stoddards' front door swung open, but I went right on shoveling snow and saving people.

"Joe DiMaggio—Ted Williams—Gil Hodges—Mickey Mantle—Yogi Berra—Babe Ruth—"

"What's all this? What's going on?" It was Mr. Stoddard. I knew his voice—deep, gruff, angry.

"—Whitey Ford—Stan Musial—Walt Disney—"

"What exactly are you doing?" Mr. Stoddard demanded.

"Shoveling," I answered. "Dizzy Dean—Paladin—Zorro—"

"Stop what you're doing and look at me."

I looked but I didn't stop. I'd already shoveled more than half the walk. I couldn't stop now. Mr. Stoddard stood like a giant in the doorway of his house, even taller than I remembered. Peeping around him was his whole family, Mrs. Stoddard, Lynette, and Lynette's little brother, Troy. They looked like they were freezing.

"Why are you doing that?" Mr. Stoddard wanted to know. "Who exactly told you to do that?"

"Nobody," I said. "It just needs it. And because I want to. Jerry Lee Lewis—Chuck Berry—Buddy Holly—and I'm doing it for free—Little Richard—the Coasters—you don't have to pay me—Davy Crockett—Annie Oakley—"

For a few seconds he didn't say anything. I could tell it wasn't the answer he'd expected.

"Well, you can stop right now," Mr. Stoddard said

at last. "It's still snowing and there's absolutely no point—"

"Why wait until it's up to the windows?" I said. "And anyway, I'm nearly done. Randolph Scott—Gene Autry —Roy Rogers—Joel McCrea—"

"Now, look—" I could tell his feet were ready to move out of the doorway toward me.

"Doug." I saw Mrs. Stoddard put a hand on her husband's arm.

"Oh, this is totally uncalled for," said Mr. Stoddard, running his fingers through his hair. "In fact, it's ridiculous."

I said, "My dad always told me never to leave a job unfinished."

I don't know where I dug up those words, but my mentioning my dad stopped Mr. Stoddard in his tracks, because for the next few minutes nobody said anything, until finally I felt the end of my shovel hit the step.

Done.

When I lifted my head, the whole family was staring at me, each with a different look.

But only one of those looks mattered.

I said, "The driveway'll take longer because it's wider. But don't worry, I'll do that for free, too."

"It won't be necessary. Just run along. Thanks for everything." Mr. Stoddard started to close the door.

"Wait!" My voice surprised even me. I'd just saved the universe from destruction and would never feel this brave again. "Please, wait." Eight eyes were on me. "What did I do that was so terrible? It's not my fault what happened next door. It's just a sad and crazy thing, and it makes me sick to think about it, especially when I think about McStew. I don't know where he is or how he is, and I wish he was here right now. I wish my dad was here. I'd tell them things I should've said. All I know for sure is, I love Lynette. I've loved her since second grade, and I'll keep on loving her, no matter what school you put her in or how far away. I just don't think it's fair, you not letting me see her until she's fifty. And if you can't handle that, then you can get somebody else to shovel your stupid driveway!" I don't know where it all came from, I just knew I meant every word. The whole family stood gawking at me, and for the first time I looked at Lynette, who had her hand over her mouth.

I said to her, "I miss your gypsy smile."

Lynette's little brother, Troy, leaned out of the doorway and said, "I built a snowman out back, wanna come see?"

"Daddy?" Lynette touched her father's sleeve.

"Doug?" said Mrs. Stoddard.

Mr. Stoddard threw his hands in the air.

"I'll get my coat on!" said Lynette. "We have a shovel in the basement."

"Scotty, aren't your ears cold?" asked Mrs. Stoddard.

"I left my earmuffs at home," I told her.

"Doug."

Mr. Stoddard went to get me a pair of his.

The driveway was hard work, especially with Troy kicking snow on areas we'd already shoveled. Once or twice his mother called him to come in the house, but he wanted to stay outside with Lynette and me.

"It's not like raking leaves, is it?" I said.

"It's better," said Lynette. She watched me the whole time we worked. Her smile never left her face.

"So how's school?" I asked.

"Okay. Well, boring, actually. I miss everyone—you especially."

Now and then her dad came to the window to stare out at us, and I waved and pointed to the earmuffs to show my thanks.

"Don't you hope it'll be like this for Christmas?" asked Lynette, squinting up at the swirling whiteness.

"I hope it'll be like this forever," I said.

More Than a
Phone Call

The last thing I wanted was to see a cop car parked in front of my house—but *two* cop cars nearly made me pee myself. The snowflakes that bounced off my cheeks and nose on the walk home were Lynette's kisses. I'd never felt so warm. When I saw those cars, I wanted to turn around and run right back to her.

Then I remembered: Mom said they'd be out to ask about McStew, what he was wearing, what he and I had talked about, and so on. I thought, well, as long as I keep the *big* secret, everything will be fine.

But two cop cars?

Next, an even more terrifying thought crossed my mind: I had sent the Shoe Guy into the kitchen where my mom was cooking. What if he really *did* carry a knife under his coat? And what if it turned out he was one of those guys who just can't stand to be rejected by

a girl? "If I can't have you, nobody will! Take this! And
this and this and *this*!"

I leaped onto the stoop and nearly tore the front
door off its hinges getting inside. "Mom!" I shouted.
"Mom!"

Mom was there, all right, but so were a lot of other
people. The house went quiet as a church when I en-
tered. And the look on everyone's face reminded me of
our house right after Dad's funeral—lots of hugging
and sniffling and low voices. Except this time there was
no hugging and two of the people were cops. Another
was the man in the black suit, the Warden. Then there
was the Shoe Guy himself, with his arm around my
mother. When Mom saw me, she rushed over and gave
me a hug. Everyone stood by and waited—but they had
no idea how long Mom's hugs could go on. Finally the
Shoe Guy came over and led her away.

The man in the suit pointed to the couch and I sat
down. For a second it looked like he was trying to smile,
but you could tell he wasn't used to it, probably because
of his job. The only thing in the room that felt like
home was the smell of Mom's cooking.

"We're here because of your neighbor." The Warden
broke the news. "Mick Stewart." As if I couldn't guess.
"Can you identify this?" To my surprise, he held out
a wrinkled envelope with my handwriting on it: "To
Mrs. Stewart. City Jail." "Is this the card you sent?" he
asked, and I nodded my head. "Would you mind taking
a look inside?"

The Warden handed me the envelope and I slipped
the card out. On the front, it had "Thank you for the
wedding gift" written in big pink letters. McStew didn't

read or write too well and he probably just grabbed the first card he saw. When I opened it, there were his words squished together in pencil:

> *Ma I dun wut Ihadta and you no he hadit*
> *cuming forall he dun to us sorry you took the*
> *blame for wut Idun yore son Mick*

My head snapped up like a puppet's and the man in the suit was staring at me, hard. "Did he tell you anything about this?"

I said, "But I thought—I mean—didn't his mother confess? Didn't she say *she* did it?"

But the Warden never answered questions, just asked them. "What I want to know is, did this boy say anything to you about killing his father?"

So here I'd been walking around with this horrible secret of McStew's when he himself had written it on a card to be mailed to the city jail. Didn't he know that people besides his mother would read it? Was he that dumb?

"Your friend was no dummy," said the Warden, answering my thoughts. "He knew this card would be read by officials before it went to his mother." He pulled up a chair and leaned so close I could smell his tobacco breath. "Now, there's no point in being untruthful—did he tell you the same thing that's written in this card?"

The two cops stood around like statues. Somewhere in the back of my mind I heard the clank of a cell door.

"I made a promise," I said, and I heard my voice crack.

"What promise?"

All at once everything spilled out, just like it did when I talked to Mr. Stoddard. "His father beat him—beat them both. So he had it coming, just like the card says. McStew hit him with a bottle to save his mother's life. I mean, what would *you* have done?" I wiped my eyes and nose with the back of my glove. I could tell Mom wanted to come to me, but the Shoe Guy held her back.

"Now, slow down," said the Warden. He put his hands on my shoulders and I felt like slapping them off.

"So are you going to arrest me?" I asked.

"You ask me that every time I come here," he said. "Tell me why I should arrest you."

"For letting a killer go free. And not telling anybody." I could barely get the words out.

The Warden took his hands off my shoulders. He glanced at the nearest cop. He said, "The individual who perpetrated the crime is in our custody. We never had any doubts that she was the one."

Now I was *good* and confused. "But the card says—"

"Seems the Stewart boy wanted you to report exactly what he told you, just as he wanted us to read this card—in order to throw the blame off his mother. It was her that did the hitting, all right. But you're right about the weapon. It was a bottle."

"Wait. You're saying McStew *wanted* to get caught?" I blinked away my tears.

"I'm saying he was trying to protect his mother, just as she protected him. What he didn't count on, I suppose, was you knowing how to keep a secret."

I sat there with snot dripping from my nose.

The Warden said, "Will you describe what Mick Stewart had on when you saw him last?"

While one of the cops jotted down what I said, I described McStew's worn-out boots and vest. I told them I was pretty sure he was wearing jeans.

"What about the shoes?" asked the man in the suit. "Your mother said you gave him some shoes."

I couldn't use the words I wanted to describe the wing-tips, what with the Shoe Guy standing there, so I just mentioned their size and color and how they had my name and phone number on the insides. "But I doubt McStew will ever put them on," I said. "They're not exactly his type."

"I wouldn't count on that," said the Warden, and all of a sudden he looked old, like someone who hadn't slept in a week. He nodded at the other cop, who handed him a brown paper bag. The Warden reached inside the bag and pulled out a burnt piece of something and stuck it under my nose. I tried to squirm away. When I forced myself to look closer, I saw it was a shoe, or what was left of a shoe, its black tongue curled up and the heel missing. It was crusty with ash, like somebody'd tried to cook it. The letters "S-c-o-t" were barely readable on the inside, and that's when horror nailed me to the couch.

"Looks like he didn't get far," said the man.

Right then, Mom took over. Tired of being shoved aside in her own living room, she broke away from the Shoe Guy and hurried to my side, nearly knocking the Warden off his chair.

"Scotty, nothing is known for sure," Mom said, taking my hand. Her eyes were puffy and her hand was sweaty. "There was a fire in some old house close to the state line. Faulty wiring—who knows? Some people died."

"Were any of them kids?" I asked.

She swallowed hard and nodded.

"McStew?" I nearly choked on his name.

"No one knows," Mom answered and narrowed her eyes at the man in the suit. "Including you."

The Warden said in a tired voice, "Ma'am, after you phoned us, we put two and two together. We already had the shoe from the fire, and—how many shoes have your son's name written on the inside?"

"But you said there were no bodies," Mom reminded him.

"I said there were no bodies that could be identified. Too badly burned. Just scraps of clothing, like this shoe here." The Warden reached inside his suit for a cigarette.

"Don't," Mom told him, and he put the cigarette back. "Scotty, listen to me. There's absolutely no proof McStew was inside that house. This could be anybody's shoe. I mean, look at it. My God, there's hardly anything left. And we can't say for sure that's your name. So how could anyone—?"

The Shoe Guy slowly made his way over to the couch. He took one look at the shoe and I could tell by his face that for a split second he thought about lying. He said, "I'm sorry," then turned away.

I shook my head and looked from face to face. "He'd be a lot farther away than the state line. He'd be out west. Wyoming."

"A boy on foot in weather like this?" The Warden shook his head.

"What about this house he supposedly was in?" Mom asked, as if she thought the whole thing was made up.

"It was for runaway kids," the Warden explained. "Unlicensed. Owned by an old couple who lost their sons in Korea. It was run-down, a disaster waiting to happen. It's tragic, and that's for certain, but it's hard not to conclude that this is our boy." He tapped the shoe with his finger and a piece of ash fell on the carpet. "We're withholding the news from his mother, at least for now. She's got a bad sickness and most likely won't make it to court."

Mom was squeezing my hand so hard it hurt. The Warden started talking like grownups do when they're about to fill your ear with some gobbledygook that's supposed to make you feel better but only ends up making *them* feel better because they get to hear themselves talk.

I sprang off the couch so suddenly that everyone jumped. "I've got to go out," I said, and sprinted toward the door.

"Scotty," Mom said.

"Wait, son," said the Warden.

"I'm not your son!" I shouted, and the next minute I was out walking. A blizzard of thoughts swirled through my brain like the whiteness that swirled through the streets and between houses. Then I heard snow crunching underfoot behind me—someone's boots trying to catch up. Pretty soon whoever it was was next to me, breathing hard.

"If somebody's hurt, it's not your fault," the Shoe

Guy wheezed, and I picked up my speed. "Everybody makes choices, and the consequences aren't always pleasant."

Maybe he meant well, maybe Mom sent him—but I wasn't in the mood for hearing speeches, especially his. But grownups never get that message. They just keep gabbing away.

"It was a decent thing you did, giving him your shoes. And remember—it's not like you could have stopped him."

No, but I could've let someone know, I thought, someone who'd have caught up with him before he burned in that fire—if that's what happened.

The Shoe Guy started falling behind. "By the way, I want to thank you for your help," he said. "I think it's going to work out. Your mom and me, I mean."

He was saying whatever popped into his head, but I knew it wouldn't last. At his age he couldn't talk and walk in the snow at the same time. And by now I was practically running.

"Remember"—I heard his voice at my back—"you need to be home by Thanksgiving." I must've been going south because he said, "If you make it all the way to Florida, how about sending us some sunshine?" From half a block away his voice still reached me. "Want to know what *I* do? I write things down. Good things, bad things—all of it. Makes me understand it better. So you might want to try that. You can write about your dad— or McStew—or anything!"

The snow finally swallowed his voice. What a windbag, I thought. And a bald windbag, at that. The Shoe Guy.

When I got back home after I don't know how long,

my feet and hands were numb and my face was raw. The only thing with any feeling left was the thing that wouldn't stop aching. At least it wasn't snowing anymore and the cops and the Shoe Guy were gone. Mom was on the phone.

"Certainly—yes, I understand," she said, and hung up. "Well, where exactly have *you* been?"

"Walking. Who was that?" I asked. I hoped there would be something new on McStew. After that burnt shoe, the news could only get better.

"Neighbors," Mom answered, flapping her hand at the phone like she was shooing it away. "I've been calling everyone I can think of to invite them for Thanksgiving dinner. But—they all have plans."

"And families," I added.

"Yes. And families." She looked at me closely. "Whose earmuffs?"

"Mr. Stoddard's. I forgot to give them back."

"Well then—sounds as if you might be making some headway with Lynette."

"Yeah, I guess."

"Good for you. Things are back being fine for Cliff and me, too," Mom said. "At least *he'll* be here for Thanksgiving."

In spite of all this happy news, neither of us was smiling.

"I suppose the Stoddards have plans, too." She sighed. "No point in calling them, would you say?"

I couldn't picture Lynette's father sitting at our table eating Thanksgiving dinner. I didn't even *want* to picture it.

"All that food." Mom shook her head. "Whatever will

we do? Freeze it, I suppose." She was carrying on a con-versation with herself.

My toes and fingers started to tingle. I took off my coat and the earmuffs.

"What a day," Mom said. "I need an aspirin."

I followed her into the kitchen.

She said, "Want to have some tomato soup with me? And a grilled-cheese sandwich?"

I nodded, even though I wasn't hungry. Our kitchen looked like it should have been attached to somebody's restaurant. Food was everywhere. Minutes later we sat across from each other at the table, both of us staring at our food.

"Mom," I said.

"You didn't kill your friend." She looked me right in the eye. "No matter what's going through your head, you've got to believe that. You know McStew. He always did things his way."

"But—"

She reached across the table and put her hand on my wrist. "You were keeping a promise and that's why you didn't tell. To someone your age, keeping a promise is more honorable than turning in a friend."

I clung to her words and forced myself to trust them. But in my mind I kept seeing McStew in the tree house on that last night. He was climbing down the rope lad-der, on his way west. I saw myself rush into the house to wake up Mom. Before he even got to the city limits, before he went into that house that caught on fire, the man in the suit brought him back. McStew was cussing me, all right, but he was alive. And safe.

My tears made little splashes in the soup. Mom took her hand off my wrist. "Scotty, if anyone's to blame, it's me."

"You?" I wiped my face with my napkin.

"I sit in this house day after day, feeling sorry for myself, lamenting my empty life, when living next door were people who got the shit kicked out of them regularly."

That got my attention. Mom never used bad words.

"How many times did we see him with bruises? I should have done something," Mom said. Then she repeated it in a lower voice, to no one.

"But you did. Remember the time they were fighting and you called the cops?"

"It takes more than a phone call. It takes—" She shook her head, as if she were trying to erase a memory. "You keep wanting to go back, replay certain things, make them turn out better. But it doesn't work. You're still left with the same rotten regrets." So Mom was doing the same thing I was. "If only I'd thought to apply for a foster-home license," she said. "If only—"

I said, "Maybe he wasn't in there. Maybe he got out."

"Maybe," she said, but like me, she was probably thinking about that shoe.

I knew there was nothing I could say to make either of us feel better, so I excused myself and went up to my room. What I really wanted was to go sit in the tree house, but it was just too cold. Instead, I stretched out on the bed and let memories of McStew sweep through my brain. I fell asleep thinking about last summer when he and I—well, mostly him—built the tree house.

I could barely picture his face. It was mixed in with the leaves of the oak.

When I woke up, it was dark out and the house smelled like fresh-baked bread. My stomach growled. Somewhere music was playing. I rubbed my eyes and wandered downstairs, where I found my mother spinning around the kitchen like some crazy top. Her arms were white with flour and the radio was turned up high. She was singing "You Are My Sunshine." When she saw me, she turned the music down and pinched my cheeks with her doughy fingers.

"It's a miracle!" Mom practically chanted. "It struck me like something out of a dream."

Just my luck, I thought—*two* parents with brain tumors.

"I can't believe I didn't think of it sooner." Mom grabbed my arm and pulled me toward the oven. She was going to shove me in, I was sure of it, just like the witch in *Hansel and Gretel*. She flung open the door and I jerked free. "Look, Scotty," Mom said with a huge smile. "Loaves. Lovely, lovely loaves."

I nodded and smiled back. I'd heard you were supposed to stay calm around crazy people. Just agree with whatever they say until someone finds a net.

Mom said, "I've discovered a path to salvation. For both of us."

"What are you talking about?"

"All this food. I knew there had to be a reason I made so much of it and why nobody accepted my invitation to dinner. This food is going to an orphanage."

"What?"

"Oh, I don't know if they still call them that—orphanages, I mean. But there are certainly establishments in this town for parentless children. And that's where we'll take the food on Thanksgiving Day."

"Are you serious?"

"It's the perfect solution," she said. "I know it won't bring back McStew, but at least it'll help other children who are as unfortunate—oh, but here. I'll bet you're starved. Have a slice of this bread and some string-bean casserole, then help me slice these apples, will you?"

When Mom got excited like that, you couldn't say no even if you wanted to. She automatically figured you felt the same way she did. A couple of summers ago she fell in love with the ocean and nothing would do but us all piling into the car and going to stay at the seashore for three days. I remember Dad complained because he had reports to write, but Mom said, "Fine, bring them along," and off we went to the ocean, Dad grumbling the entire way.

I helped Mom in the kitchen all evening, peeling, paring, washing, fetching. Normally I would've minded missing my TV shows, but in a weird sort of way it was fun. Mom sang and whistled and even told a joke or two. She was suddenly somebody different, like in that movie, *Invasion of the Body Snatchers*. And all because of some hungry, homeless kids she didn't even know. It was true I couldn't get as worked up about it as she was, but it was worth doing just to see her happy. And I remembered how good it made me feel when I took McStew food.

The next morning, Sunday, I was awakened by someone shaking my shoulder. "Up and at 'em, soldier," Mom said. "I need you to come down and watch the oven while I run to the store. Thank goodness I had chains put on the tires last week—whew! All that snow." She smelled like five or six different flavors and was talking a mile a minute. I wondered if she'd even slept. It was useless for me to roll back over—the Mad Baker had me in her clutches. "You'll be thrilled to hear I called three different shelters that will accept our services on Thanksgiving. But of course that means I have to go buy extra turkeys—big ones, at that."

While I sat at the kitchen table eating a waffle (there was barely enough room for me, with all that food), I began to worry that Mom was going overboard. I hated to sound selfish when I was supposed to be helping others, but what if there wasn't enough left for us? It's not like we were millionaires. I brought it up while helping her haul groceries in from the car.

"Oh, don't even think about it," Mom said, her cheeks rosy from the cold. "One thing about your father. He had a terrific attitude toward money. He saved every penny and left it all to me. That's what I call a thoughtful husband. Here, put these sweet potatoes over there. Oh, and you might as well get busy dicing onions. They'll clear your sinuses. Did you finish your breakfast?" She didn't even take off her coat before she was buzzing around like some tortured insect, and she never stopped talking. "Good day to stay inside and cook," Mom said. "It's too cold to be playing out there in that tree house."

It wasn't the tree house I had on my mind. It was Lynette Stoddard. I had a great excuse for going over to her house—I had to return her father's earmuffs.

"And don't worry about earmuffs," Mom said. "I'm

sure the Stoddards have plenty extras." She surprised me by turning the radio to a rock-and-roll station and even hummed along with the songs. "This music isn't *all* bad," she admitted, "although singing lessons wouldn't hurt. Some of them go so fast I can't understand a word they say."

"You're not supposed to," I told her. "It's the beat that counts."

"Oh, I beg to differ," said Mom. "Lyrics are half the song. If you can't hear the words, that's like eating food you can't taste."

Food. Everything lately had to do with food.

I said, "How are you planning to get all this stuff where it's going? We'll need a moving van."

"My goodness—you're right! Do you know I never gave that a thought? Our car's too small, isn't it? Unless of course we make several trips, and who wants to do that on snowy roads? Hmm. Let's see. Who do we know who has a big car?"

"The Stoddards," I said. "They have a station wagon."

"The Stoddards—exactly!" said Mom. "I'll call them right now."

"But if they won't come here to eat, what makes you think they'll want to go to an orphanage on Thanksgiving?"

"You never know until you ask," Mom answered, licking her fingers. "If they can lend earmuffs, they can lend a station wagon."

"They'll be in church now," I said, glancing at the clock.

"Then I'll call later. What's the point of going to

church if you don't apply what you learn? That's what I'll tell Doug Stoddard if he tries to refuse."

"Please don't," I said. All I could think of was how Mr. Stoddard would just get all riled up again and stop me from seeing Lynette. Why'd I have to go and open my mouth about the station wagon?

But Mom was determined. "When the Stoddards sent a card after Frank died, they wrote a note saying that if ever they could be of any help, to be sure and give them a call. I still have that card and I don't mind waving it in their faces."

"Well, at least talk to *Mrs.* Stoddard," I said.

"I'll talk to whoever will listen."

That was one conversation I didn't want to hear. I slipped out of the room when Mom called the Stoddards. I wondered if Mr. Stoddard would now send Lynette to a private school in Alaska. But when I went back in the kitchen Mom said, "Everything's set. We'll have the use of their wagon. Doug agreed to drive."

"No kidding. You must've talked to Lynette's mom."

"No, I talked to her dad."

"Now I know you're kidding."

"Doug Stoddard is a pharmacist, don't forget, a healer. Just because he doesn't approve of certain individuals dating his daughter doesn't mean he wants to see children go hungry."

"What did you say to him?"

"Oh, I think I might have mentioned how good it would be for his reputation if people in the community knew he spent Thanksgiving feeding needy children— and how bad it would be if he didn't."

"So you blackmailed him."

"I did no such a thing."

"Did he say anything about Lynette?" I asked.

"Who's Lynette?" Mom handed me a bowl of batter.

On Monday I was actually glad to go to school just to get out of the kitchen. All the kids were happy because it was only a three-day week. But once again they pestered me about McStew. It had been in Sunday's paper about that house fire, and my name was mentioned in connection with the shoes, "believed to be worn by Mick Stewart at the time of the fire." People treated me like a hero because I'd given McStew some stupid shoes I didn't want in the first place. A hero was the last thing I felt like, and hearing McStew's name only made me miserable. I was miserable enough as it was because I knew I was going to spend Thanksgiving riding around with Mom, Mr. Stoddard, and the Shoe Guy. I didn't mind feeding hungry kids. But being cooped up in a car with those three? Jeez.

"Too bad about McStew," said Corky Perkins. "Now me, I'd have hauled my sweet butt out of there at the first sign of smoke—but not McStew. Oh, no, not him. He had to stick around and make an *ash* of himself, haw, haw."

"Go to hell," I said, and gave Corky a shove.

"Boy, have *I* got a great idea," said Chip Keller at lunch. "It'll make you wish you'd thought of it."

I just walked away. I didn't want to talk to anyone except Lynette. If only she were there, things would be fine.

Miss Twilley held me back at the end of the day. I

thought, oh, no, things are going to get even worse. But she said, "Mick Stewart was indeed fortunate to have you for a friend." I liked her for saying that. But it crossed my mind that she was probably feeling guilty, too. On some days McStew came to school with a black eye and he'd sit in the back of the class where no one paid attention to him. Everyone thought he was dumb.

Mom had told me to hurry home after school so I could help out some more. I was thinking of asking her if I could stay home for the two days before Thanksgiving, but I knew she'd never go for that. Suddenly, scrubbing pots and pans was more appealing than hearing everybody talk about McStew. I couldn't believe it. When he was alive, it seemed like McStew was always getting me into some kind of mess. Now that he was possibly dead, nothing had changed.

To my surprise, Mom was asleep on the couch when I walked in the door. She'd finally tuckered herself out. One shoe lay on the floor and the other dangled from her toes. Toby was curled up close to her head. I held my hand close to his face.

"Hi, Toby," I whispered, and although he didn't run away, he looked at me as if to say, "Who told *you* my name?"

When I covered Mom with an afghan, she didn't move a muscle.

The kitchen sink was piled high with dirty dishes. I was nearly through washing them when the phone rang. It was Chip. He said, "You didn't stick around to hear my idea."

"Not interested," I said and hung up.

The phone rang again and I wouldn't have answered it except I didn't want it to wake up Mom.

"He's not dead," said Chip.

"Who's not dead?"

"Who do you think? He got away."

"How do you know?"

"Don't you get it? Someone else was wearing those shoes."

"Chip—"

"Think about it. McStew was probably in the house, all right, but being the kind of person he is, he left the shoes with some other kid who needed them even worse. Or this. Maybe the house caught on fire and McStew tossed the shoes into the blaze so people would just *think* he was dead and quit looking for him."

"That's crazy," I said.

"Is it? Scotty, you knew McStew better than anyone. Doesn't it sound like something he'd do?"

It did.

"So there you are," said Chip. "The Gypsy Bandit strikes again! It'll be a chapter in my book."

I saw Mom standing in the doorway of the kitchen and I hung up.

She yawned and said, "Who keeps calling?"

"Chip," I answered. "He's being a nuisance."

"Nothing new there—oh, man, did I ever sleep! Hey, thanks for doing the dishes, you're a sweetheart." Mom started to give me a hug, when the phone rang again.

I snatched it off the hook and yelled, "Go away!" but it was the Shoe Guy.

Suddenly Mom was wide awake. I signaled to her that I was going out to the tree house and she waved at me while chattering with her boyfriend.

The tree house felt like an igloo, but my mind was racing so fast I couldn't be bothered with the cold.

What if Chip was right?

But Chip was *never* right.

But what if he was, this once?

In my hand was the stone, the "bullet" that killed Reese. Ever since McStew gave it to me I'd carried it in my shirt pocket, remembering to take it out each night so it wouldn't end up in the wash. I sat there and thought about McStew and the way he was. He loved the idea of people jumping in the way of bullets or arrows to save others, as Reese had done. Didn't he come out and confess to the cops that *he* was the one who stole Old Man Miller's paint? And didn't he try to take the blame for killing his father in order to keep his mother out of the electric chair? It would be just like him, then, to give those shoes to some kid who didn't have any, as Chip had said. Not only that, I couldn't picture McStew walking west in wing-tips.

So he had to have been in that house, all right, because the shoes were there. The question was, did he get out before the house burned down? I held the stone tight, as if to squeeze out an answer.

That evening Mom kept me busy knocking on neighbors' doors to borrow extra plates and covered dishes. Everyone looked surprised, but all I said was, "Family reunion." Which was a laugh, because all my living relatives could've fit around the kitchen table, with room to spare.

When I got back from one of those trips, Mom handed me the phone. "Friend of yours," she said.

"Why couldn't you just tell him I'm not here?" I whispered, but she kept holding the phone out.

"Hello?" I said.

"Hi, Scotty."

"Lynette!"

"Guess what? I get to go, too."

"That's great! Go where?"

"With you to the children's homes on Thanksgiving. Your mom talked my folks into letting me."

I grinned at my mother, who pretended not to notice.

The next day people pretty much left me alone—except of course Chip. Chip was everywhere.

"I just know it'll be a best-seller," he kept saying. "And think of the movie! But I need you to fill in some details." He had a notepad and pencil ready to go.

"Make them up," I told him, "like you do everything else."

That night Chip called me at home.

"Not you again," I said.

"As usual, you miss the point. Scotty, this could make us both rich. Most kids have heroes who are movie stars or ball players, but this is different. This is a real live kid—uh, well, we hope."

"McStew isn't a hero. He's just some poor guy whose family fell apart and he had to run away."

But Chip wasn't listening. He said, "Instead of calling it *The Legend of the Gypsy Bandit*, I can change it to *Scotty and the Gypsy Bandit*. Or even *Durango and the Gypsy Bandit*. Isn't that what he used to call you? What do you think?"

"What do I think? I'll tell you what I think. I think I'll write my own book."

I hung up the phone and went to my room. I remembered what the Shoe Guy said about writing things down. It helps you understand it better. There was stuff buzzing around in my brain with no place to go. Just to see what it felt like, I took out a pencil and some paper and began to write. I wrote about my dad and my mom and the tree house and McStew. And of course Lynette. I even wrote about Chip. A couple of hours later, when Mom came in to tell me good night, I was still writing.

Thanksgiving

Early Wednesday evening the phone rang twice, and both times I expected it to be Chip, but no one was there.

"Sometimes when people realize they've dialed the wrong number they just hang up," said Mom, poking a fork into her latest turkey roasting in the oven.

"But twice?"

"It happens."

"What if it was McStew?"

She gave me a funny look.

"Our phone number was in those shoes, remember?"

"The shoes got burned," Mom reminded me.

"Even so," I said, "the last thing I told him was to give me a call when he got out west. So maybe this is his way of letting me know."

"How like him to use a secret code," said Mom, but I

could tell she didn't believe it. She snapped the oven door shut.

"Well, we'll see if it happens a third time," I said, and I nearly jumped out of my skin when the phone rang. I snatched it off the hook. "McStew, where are you?"

Mr. Stoddard's frosty voice said, "May I please speak with your mother?"

Mom cleared her throat and spoke into the phone. "Yes, Doug—oh, I'd say about nine or nine-thirty—the earlier the better, yes, I agree—see you then."

I helped myself to a slice of turkey off a covered plate and wandered into the living room to sit on the couch. Toby scrambled out from beneath it and darted up the stairs. Halfway he paused and peeped at me through the rails. I tore off a hunk and set it on the floor by my feet. "For you," I said.

He looked at the turkey and licked his lips.

"Mmm, good." I licked my own lips.

His eyes never left that turkey. With my shoe I pushed it away from me, and Toby came back down the stairs. He started creeping toward the meat as if he thought he was invisible and I had no idea he was in the room. When he was only an inch or two away he stopped, and his yellow eyes looked up at me.

"It's for you," I told him. "Honest."

But all he did was sit there, switching his big gray tail.

I said, "I know. You're waiting for a side order of baseball cards, right? Well, here." I reached into my shirt pocket and pulled out two cards which I had doubles of. I very slowly set them down next to the turkey.

"Okay, so what's the catch?" Toby seemed to ask.

"No catch. I'm just thankful to have a big gray cat in the house," I said. I got up from the couch, again very slowly, and walked away. When I looked over my shoulder, he was bent over the turkey, munching away.

"There. Are you happy?" I spoke to McStew, wherever he was.

Before going to bed that night, I said to Mom, "It's not fair if McStew's dead."

"Life's not fair," she said. "Sooner or later you were bound to find that out."

It wasn't what I wanted to hear.

The next morning broke cold and dark, as usual. When I looked out my bedroom window, the tree house made me think of a huge Christmas ornament stuck among the branches of the oak. I thought of things to be thankful for, besides a big gray cat: Lynette was coming over—well, that was it, mostly. Lynette was coming over. Plus, Lynette's mom had insisted that after we did our good deeds we should all come to the Stoddards' house for dinner. Even the Shoe Guy. I couldn't keep from wondering how she'd talked her husband into *that*.

Downstairs, the doorbell rang, and I heard the Shoe Guy's voice. He and Mom were hugging, probably, and maybe even kissing. But what the heck, I thought. Let them do what they wanted. After all, who was it that helped bring them back together?

I practiced making movie-star faces in the mirror.

"Scotty," Mom called up to me. "Are you ready?"

"On my way!" I answered. I was doing a pretty good James Dean.

Just as I got to the bottom of the stairs, the station

wagon carrying Lynette and her father pulled up in front of our house. Lynette had on a red snowsuit and a red cap with a silver bell on it. Her butterscotch-colored hair was tied back in a ponytail. Just the sight of her breath puffing up our walk made me feel like fainting. And I remembered something the Shoe Guy said: "There will always be some girl's smile to keep you awake at night. If you're lucky." I suddenly understood what he meant about going into Mac's Diner to watch my mom wait on customers.

When I opened the door, there was Mr. Stoddard's big old self blocking my view of his daughter. *He* made me feel like fainting, too.

"Doug—good morning!" Mom breezed into the room drying her hands on a towel, and for a second I thought she was going to hug him.

"Is everything set?" asked Mr. Stoddard, all business.

"Good morning, Lynette," said Mom, peeping around Mr. Stoddard. "Happy Thanksgiving."

"Happy Thanksgiving," Lynette answered, but it was me she was looking at.

"Hello, hello, hello!" the Shoe Guy's jolly voice rolled into the room. With his rosy cheeks and bald head, he looked like somebody off a Christmas card. "Aha!" he pointed at Lynette. "You obviously are Scott's lovely lady friend."

This was followed by dead silence. Mr. Stoddard pulled his daughter close to him. I felt like rolling myself into the carpet. More than that, I felt like rolling the Shoe Guy into the carpet and rolling him out the door and into the street.

"Well"—Mom clapped her hands together—"I guess we'd better hop to it. Our first stop will be the Sunnyside Shelter for Boys."

For the next fifteen minutes the five of us were like an army of ants, passing cardboard boxes filled with covered dishes and roasting pans and plastic containers to one another and loading the back of the Stoddards' station wagon. Mom had it all worked out. We were to hit three different places she had called, and the food was divided up in the kitchen according to how many kids were in each place. The one thing she hadn't figured out was how to keep everything warm.

"Ovens, Marie. They'll have ovens," the Shoe Guy assured her.

When it was time to leave, I tried worming my way into the seat next to Lynette. Mr. Stoddard drove, naturally, and he saw to it that Lynette sat up front between him and Mom, who gave directions. I sat behind Mom, next to the Shoe Guy. A roasted turkey rested on the seat between us. Everything else was in the space behind the seats.

"Just us turkeys back here, huh, Scott?" the Shoe Guy said to me, and I rolled my eyes.

"Now, drive slow," Mom said, "so the food won't jostle around."

"Well, of course I'll drive slow," said Mr. Stoddard. "Don't you see how icy these roads are?" He wasn't in a good mood to begin with, and being told how to drive didn't help.

"Hey, Scott," said the Shoe Guy, "how about passing me another turkey leg?"

Mom swung around in her seat. "Don't you *dare*."

"Just kidding, Marie, just kidding," the Shoe Guy chuckled, and he winked at me. Nothing was going to sour *his* mood.

The food smelled great, and it reminded my stomach that it hadn't eaten any breakfast. Now and then Lynette turned to show me her smile and I lost my appetite. I wanted to touch her ponytail and rub it between my fingers, but her father's face in the rearview mirror changed my mind.

Earlier in the week Mom had called the three homes we were going to, to find out how many kids were there. I'd asked her a million questions.

"Who's in these places, anyway?"

"I don't know. Kids who've been abandoned or kicked out of their homes. Kids who've been abused. Runaways, too, I suppose."

"Like McStew?"

"Yes, like McStew."

"But who'd kick out their own kid?" I wanted to know.

Mom just shook her head.

I remember going to bed that night thinking Dad had died but I still had Mom. But what if Mom died? What would happen to me then? Would I be put in one of those places? No, I'd probably go stay with Uncle Don and Aunt Sue. But what if they didn't want me? They had a new baby, and there was no law saying they had to take me in. I shivered under the covers.

The Sunnyside Shelter for Boys was nothing like what I expected. In spite of its name, I pictured some broken-down old church with dozens of dirty kids climbing out the windows and maybe a couple of sour-faced old biddies (Mrs. Mackley and Miss Twilley) chasing after them with rolling pins. Instead, it was a regular house, kind of small, and the person who came out to meet us was a man not much older than Dad. "God cough bless you, cough," were the first words out of his mouth. He was puffing away on a cigarette. "I'm Stanley Bryce. You must be Mrs. Hansen, cough, cough."

"Yes, and this is Mr. Douglas Stoddard of Stoddard Pharmacy." Mom practically shoved Lynette's father in the man's face.

"Yes, of course, I know it well," said the man, hacking into the palm of his hand.

"Sounds like he could *use* a pharmacy." The Shoe Guy nudged me.

Mom didn't bother introducing the rest of us. Instead, she barked orders to start taking stuff out of the car.

"Watch your step on this sidewalk, folks," warned Mr. Bryce. "The boys salted it down, but you can't be too careful."

Inside, there was very little heat. Nine or ten boys were huddled together on a tiled floor with blankets wrapped around their shoulders, watching TV. Something was wrong with the set and the picture blinked on and off, but the boys didn't seem to care. It was like an old folks' home.

Mr. Bryce got their attention. "Lookit here, everybody—Thanksgiving!"

The boys' faces all turned as if pulled by strings. And in the next minute they clambered around us, eager to see what was in the boxes.

"Whoa, whoa, just give us a second." Mr. Bryce waved them away with his cigarette. "Go back to the TV. We'll call you."

But the boys didn't want to go back to the TV. They wanted to follow their noses into those boxes. All I could think of was the time my family spent a few days at the ocean and Mom and I walked the beach feeding seagulls. Flocks of them swarmed around us as if they hadn't eaten in weeks.

I followed Lynette into a little kitchen area not much warmer than the room the TV was in. A boy about ten years old was sitting at a table eating cereal. He wore a bandage over his nose. Mr. Bryce told us to put the boxes on the table while he rounded up some plates.

"Sandy here's our late riser," Mr. Bryce explained without smiling. "We call him Mr. Made-in-the-Shade, isn't that right, Sandy? Mr. The-World-Owes-Me-a-Living."

The boy ignored him. He said to me, "Soon's I'm done eating, I'll show you around."

"Huh?"

"Just watch out for Marvin Messick. He swipes underwear. Do you smoke?"

We couldn't get out of there fast enough. On our way to the car Lynette said, "That boy thought you were moving in."

"He asked me if I smoked," I told her.

"I don't think I can go into another place like that," she said with a shiver.

We all sat in the car waiting for the Shoe Guy, who stood in the doorway of the house talking to Mr. Bryce and jotting things down on a piece of paper.

"So what's he doing, writing a book?" Mr. Stoddard said impatiently, just as I was thinking about what to write in my own book.

On the drive back to the house, nobody said much, not even the Shoe Guy. Finally Mom broke the silence. "We just did this incredibly wonderful thing. So why don't any of us feel better?"

"I could have told you it wouldn't be pretty," said Mr. Stoddard. "Those kids—" He didn't finish his sentence, and we drove through the snowy streets in silence. Like Lynette, I didn't care to go into any more of those places.

Back at the house, we carried cartons of food out to the station wagon like they were tiny caskets on their way to the cemetery. When we were ready to get back in the car, the Shoe Guy said, "Stop. Wait. Listen." We all looked at him. "Folks, excuse me for saying so, but we're going about this all wrong. It's fine to take food to these kids, but we should be doing something extra."

"What do you mean, extra?" Mr. Stoddard frowned. I could tell he just wanted to get on with it.

"What are you getting at, Cliff?" asked Mom.

"I'm saying how about we inject a little personality into this next visit? Maybe if we acted more like human beings and less like delivery boys, we'd feel better about what we're doing." He looked at each one of us. "In other words, why not spend a little time with these kids?"

"What do you hope to prove by that?" said Mr. Stoddard.

"I don't especially want to prove anything. I just want to feel human."

Mom said, "Well, I think it's a marvelous idea! Do you know that at that boy's shelter we were in such a hurry to get away I don't believe one of us thought to say 'Happy Thanksgiving.' I know I didn't."

"That's my point," said the Shoe Guy.

Mr. Stoddard glanced at his wristwatch. "Great. Just great," he grunted.

All at once, Mom had reached her limit. I could hear it in her voice, had heard it many times in my life. She said, "I'll tell you what, Doug. We'll take it from here."

"I beg your pardon?"

"You are hereby relieved of duty—you and Lynette. You helped us with the first delivery and I thank you, but from here on out Cliff and Scotty and I will manage just fine in two cars. So if you'll help us transfer everything—"

"Now hold on. I never said—"

"Oh, you didn't have to—*Ebenezer*," Mom interrupted him, and her breath looked like smoke from a rifle. "I realize you're an exceptional parent and I'm sure you're an example we could all stand here and learn from. But today isn't about you. It's about kids who don't *have* parents, and if you can't see that, then you're here for the wrong reasons." She shook her head. "It's my fault for bullying you into this. My God, I don't even like you! I just wanted the use of your station wagon."

I thought, aw, jeez, there goes my love life.

"Now just hold your horses," said Mr. Stoddard, who

wasn't used to being talked to that way. "Aren't you forgetting that you accepted my wife's invitation to dinner?"

"I didn't say I didn't like your wife. I said I didn't like you."

The rest of us stood around, looking embarrassed. Lynette and I stared past each other. A car rolled by with some of our neighbors from down the street. They honked, waved, cranked down a window, and called out, "Happy Thanksgiving!"

Mr. Stoddard said, "Oh, let's just forget all this! Everybody get back in the damn car."

"What kind of attitude is that on Thanksgiving?" Mom asked.

"Okay, will everybody *please* get back in the damn car," said Mr. Stoddard.

"That's more like it," said Mom. "Cheerful attitudes all around."

We all piled into the station wagon, same seating as before, another turkey between the Shoe Guy and me.

"Wow, Mom!" I whispered in my mother's ear.

"Yeah. Well." That's all she had to say.

The Sister Mary Windsor Home for Girls was in an old barn near the edge of town. Or at least it used to be a barn. Someone—Sister Mary Windsor, I guess—took away the horses and cows and stuff and put in rooms and walls and beds for homeless girls. When we drove up to it, the Shoe Guy said he felt that he was entering a Norman Rockwell painting. There were snow-covered trees all around and a frozen stream with a footbridge. The place was run by nuns.

Lynette whispered to her dad as we got out of the car. I heard him say, "Sure, honey. You just sit tight until we're done. Will you be warm enough?"

Mom went up a dirt path to the building's front door while the Shoe Guy, Mr. Stoddard, and I started unloading. Lynette stayed in the car and I wished I could crawl in next to her.

Pretty soon a flock of nuns came fluttering down the path with Mom in the lead.

"Lovely—absolutely lovely!" the head nun sang out. "You have no idea what a godsend you are. The Bishop had to cut our funding this year, so—" We didn't have to do a thing. The nuns took everything from us and carried it in themselves. There were three of them and I couldn't tell them apart.

The girls inside the "barn" were livelier than the boys at the Sunnyside Shelter had been. Everybody was doing something. Some were playing checkers, a couple sat and sewed, and two were having a fistfight. Three others stood around a dented old piano singing "What a Friend We Have in Jesus" while a rosy-cheeked nun pounded away on broken keys. It sounded awful. The furniture was patched and stained, but nobody seemed to mind. The place had a minty smell.

I went with Mom and the nuns into a big steamy kitchen with boiling pots. "It helps vaporize the air," one very old nun explained. She reminded me of one of the witches in *Macbeth* I'd seen on TV.

After the food was put away we went back to the main room, where the girls were—twelve or thirteen of them, all different ages. Mr. Stoddard stood with his hands stuffed in his pockets. The girls around the piano were singing "The Old Rugged Cross." A nun had broken up the two who'd been fighting and now they were praying.

"Hey, I know you. You're Rupert Blanding's brother," a serious-looking girl in pigtails said to me.

"No, I'm not."

"Yes, you are."

"But I'm not."

"Then how come you look like him?"

"I don't even have a brother," I said.

"Tell him Lydia LaSalle still wears his ring." She held out a finger. On it was a ring from a cereal box.

"I'll tell him," I said and went to stand next to Mom. Like Mr. Stoddard, I wasn't keen on sticking around. All those girls. There was only one girl who mattered to me, and she was out in the car.

"*Now*, what's he doing?" asked Mr. Stoddard, gazing across the room.

I looked to where his eyes went and there was the Shoe Guy, down on his hands and knees, making sounds like a donkey.

"Have you lost your mind?" Mr. Stoddard called to him.

On the Shoe Guy's back were two little girls, squealing their heads off. "Free donkey rides, free donkey rides!" he brayed, then went romping around the room. A guy his age. Mom laughed and clapped her hands.

"He needs a counselor," said Mr. Stoddard.

Girls were lined up to get on the Shoe Guy's back, and Mom said, "There's room over there for one more donkey."

"Not likely," Mr. Stoddard told her.

"Oh, but I bet you used to do things like that with Lynette."

"She's my daughter."

"I wonder whose daughters *they* are?" asked Mom.

After the smaller kids had had their donkey rides, the Shoe Guy did magic tricks. All the girls in the place made a circle around him. Even the nuns looked on. First he juggled the oranges and apples we'd brought. Then he turned hairpins and buttons into quarters. He made one girl's Raggedy Ann doll disappear then reappear, and made ribbons fly through the air like birds.

"How's he doing that?" I asked.

"He used to be in the circus," Mom answered.

"Him?"

"He was a clown."

"You never told me that."

"You never asked."

The Shoe Guy—a circus clown! I couldn't take my eyes away.

"He's actually not too bad," Mr. Stoddard admitted.

"I know he'll be thrilled," said Mom, winking at me.

The Shoe Guy was now turning himself into strange animals, twisting his arms and legs around like Silly Putty and making his face into a mask. His nose, always red, looked like a clown's. The girls were laughing and clapping and jumping up and down.

All but one. She was about eight. I noticed her standing by herself, by the window. When I walked over, she was hugging a broken Barbie doll with a Band-Aid on its leg. The girl's mouth was turned down at the corners.

"What's wrong?" I asked.

"She looks so sad," said the girl.

"Who?"

She pointed out the window, down the path, to the station wagon where Lynette sat alone. "Like she doesn't have a friend in the world." Before I could explain, the girl rushed out the door.

"Scotty," Mom called to me. "We're going now."

The nuns and the girls were still standing around the Shoe Guy, applauding. He took many bows and said, "Stay tuned, folks! This Saturday, on our stage, for your enjoyment—the splendiferous, stupendous antics of Jocko the Clown!" Everyone applauded even harder.

"Cliff, are you sure you want to come back here on Saturday?" I heard Mom speak to him in a low voice.

"Sure. If you'll come with me." The Shoe Guy grinned. "It's my day off."

The girls naturally didn't want to see us leave, but Mom explained that we had another stop to make. The nuns couldn't thank us enough. A couple of them walked us to the car. For a minute I thought they'd get in and go with us. Once again we had to wait for the Shoe Guy, who wrote things down on a piece of paper while talking to the head nun.

When we got in the car, something was wrong with Lynette.

"What is it, honey?" said her father. "Are you sick?"

At first she didn't answer. She just sat there and shook.

"My God," said Mr. Stoddard, cranking the engine, "we've got to get her to a doctor!"

"Don't leave without Cliff," said Mom.

Lynette said, "I'm not sick." Cradled in her arms was

the broken Barbie. "She looked like she was freezing—but she ran out to give me this."

"Who? Who gave you that?" asked Mr. Stoddard.

"A girl from in there," Lynette answered, pointing.

"Well, we've got to give it back. It's probably her only doll, and you've got a whole closetful."

"Doug," Mom interrupted. "That girl, whoever she is, wanted Lynette to have it."

"Yes, but—"

"So here's an idea," said Mom. "Cliff and I are coming back on Saturday for Cliff to do some more of his clown act. Why not let Lynette come with us? She can bring the girl one of her Barbies, seeing as how she has so many."

Lynette cheered right up. "Can I, Daddy? Can I?"

"Oh, I don't know about *that*," said Mr. Stoddard.

"Well, you think about it," said Mom. "I know you'll make the right decision—as always."

Just then the Shoe Guy came puffing down the path. He slid into the back seat next to me, breathing hard. "Sorry, folks—whew! Jocko's out of shape."

"Cliff, what exactly is it that you keep writing down?" Mom asked as Mr. Stoddard put the car in gear.

"Shoe sizes," the Shoe Guy answered, and Mom smiled.

When we got to the house for the last load of food, I heard Lynette say to her father, "Daddy, I want to go in with you this next time." She was still holding the broken Barbie doll.

"Sweetheart, it's just too upsetting," said Mr. Stoddard. "You're better off waiting in the car."

"But I want to. I really want to," said Lynette. And to herself I heard her say, "They're kids, just like me."

While the others were out front loading stuff into the station wagon, I stayed in the kitchen to help Mom. I said, "Can I ask you something?"

"Shoot."

"Why'd Mr. Ragland quit being a circus clown to be—the Shoe Guy?"

"It's a long story," Mom said, taking cole slaw out of the refrigerator.

"But I want to know."

"All right, here's the short version. He and his wife had a clown act together."

"You mean he's married?"

"Was. They toured together—until she left him for another clown."

I couldn't help it; I broke out laughing.

"What's so funny?"

"A clown leaving a clown for another clown? Come on. You don't think that's funny?"

"Well, it's what happened, and there was nothing comical about it. He was heartbroken. She meant everything to him," said Mom. "For a while it destroyed his sense of humor. He quit the circus, took all his savings and started a totally different life—shoes."

"And he told you all this?"

"When people learn to care about each other, they talk about things close to their hearts," said Mom.

"Wow. I never knew."

She stopped what she was doing and put her arm around me. "Scotty, you've got a good heart and I'm proud that you're my son, but between the two of us we could fill a book with things you never knew."

I thought about how those things were going to go into *my* book. And I remembered something the Shoe Guy said to me that day he came up in the tree house and we talked about my dad: "There are more ways to lose somebody than through death."

Our next and final stop was the Lord Calvert Boys' Home, which, Mom said, used to be a warehouse for old tires. On the outside it still looked like a warehouse for old tires. But inside it was pretty nice—nicer than the first two places. For one thing, the walls were painted with pictures of animals and the paint didn't have cracks. The furniture looked new.

"We've been lucky," said the owner, a man who was shorter than me. He was shaped funny, too, like a pear with clothes. "The right sponsors, the right business connections—nothing quite takes the place of money. Like the man says, money talks."

"Why's he so short?" I whispered to Lynette. "Is he a midget?"

"No, I think he's a dwarf," Lynette whispered back.

"The kids think I'm an elf." The little man, who had excellent hearing, laughed, and Lynette and I were embarrassed. "But that's fine with me. They relate better to someone their own size. I used to be in a home like this myself, you know. Like the man says, you have to put back in what you take out." His bowed legs carried him over to us and he reached out his little fingers to shake our hands. "Pleased to meet you. I'm Lord Calvert, but just call me L.C. Everyone does."

After we'd brought all the food in, Lord Calvert surprised us by grabbing hold of Mr. Stoddard's hand and pulling him into the main room, where the boys were playing games and talking to two other workers, who were normal size.

"Hey, everyone, look who's here!" Lord Calvert shouted. "I want you all to meet my twin brother!" All faces stared up at Lynette's father, who was over six feet tall. "When we were kids, nobody could tell us apart. Not even Ma."

Some of the kids giggled and others just shook their heads. "Aw, L.C., who're you kiddin'? You know he ain't your brother."

"That's what you think! Every time I did something wrong, he got the whipping." Everyone laughed, while Mr. Stoddard just looked confused. "We'd take turns going to school. The teachers were so dumb they never found out." That got some hoots. "Thank God for twin brothers, right, little bro?" Lord Calvert thumped Mr. Stoddard on the knee and told us, "He was voted 'Bro Most Likely to Grow.'" Then before anyone knew it, the little guy was climbing Lynette's dad like he was a tree. He sat on Mr. Stoddard's shoulders, his tiny legs strapped around his neck, pretending his hands were binoculars, shouting, "I can see Arkansas! I can see Arkansas!" The kids went wild. Lynette covered her mouth.

Lord Calvert said, "Come on, Bro! We got to lead this parade." And he sang, "Sound off!"

And the kids repeated, "Sound off!" Then Mr. Stoddard's long legs moved forward. Everyone joined in behind him, forming a line, their hands on the hips of the person in front.

Lord Calvert sang, "I don't know but I've been told—"

And the others sang, "I don't know but I've been told—"

"My life's headed down a different road!"

"My life's headed down a different road!"

"Sound off!"

"Sound off!"

"One, two, three, four—*sound off*!"

Mom said to the Shoe Guy, "Looks like you've met your match."

The Shoe Guy agreed. "He's a bigger man than me."

"But not any better," said Mom, taking his arm in hers.

The Shoe Guy and Mom and Lynette and I hooked onto the end of the line, and with Mr. Stoddard and Lord Calvert in the lead, we marched all over that warehouse.

"I just can't believe this." Lynette giggled. "My dad's leading a parade!"

Lord Calvert sang, "I don't know but I've been told—"

"I don't know but I've been told—"

"Your grandma's cow is getting old!"

"Your grandma's cow is getting old!"

"And if you pick your neighbor's toes—"

"And if you pick your neighbor's toes—"

"Remember not to pick your nose!"

"Remember not to pick your nose!"

"Sound off!"

"Sound off!"

The parade finally came to a stop, and before leaping down off Mr. Stoddard's shoulders, Lord Calvert said, "How's the weather down there, little bro?"

"Fine, so long as I don't get peed on," answered Mr. Stoddard, and everyone cracked up.

"Scotty, did you hear that?" said Lynette, squeezing my hand. "My daddy made a joke. He made a joke!"

I figured it probably wasn't a joke. He really didn't want to get peed on. But all I cared about was that Lynette's hand was in mine. And my heart was shouting, "I can see Arkansas!"

After that, the Shoe Guy sailed into action. The stage was set. He and Lord Calvert made quite a pair. You'd have thought they'd known each other all their lives, leapfrogging over each other and trading friendly insults back and forth.

Lord Calvert: "Is that your head, or did someone lay an egg?"

The Shoe Guy: "*You* did—with that joke!"

They used Lynette's dad as the straight man, chasing all around him and crawling between his legs. He didn't even look like he minded—too much. But what choice did he have?

Once the Shoe Guy even got me in on the act. "Oho, so you thought you'd get away *Scott-free*, did you?" I was surprised by his strength when he snatched me away from Lynette and lifted me off the ground. "Free kid! Free kid! Anybody want a free kid?"

"Did you say 'free kid,' or 'freak id'?" said Lord Calvert.

"I don't think they got that one," replied the Shoe

Guy. He held me up to Mr. Stoddard, who passed me on to others. Suddenly I was being handed over the heads of every kid in the place, like a package being delivered to who knows where. The next thing I knew, I was back standing next to Lynette.

A boy with a two-inch pompadour was talking to her. He said, "So would you like to be my girl?"

"Oh, I'd love to," said Lynette, "but"—she took my hand in hers—"I *have* a boyfriend."

"You sure are lucky," the boy said to me.

"I can see Arkansas," I told him.

"Okay, who's next?" shouted the Shoe Guy, and his eyes fell on my mother, who tried to hide.

We stayed longer than we'd planned. When finally everyone settled down and the kids were ready to eat, Lord Calvert invited us to join them, but Mom said we had to go. I knew she was afraid there might not be enough to go around.

"Don't worry—Jocko will return!" said the Shoe Guy. "Marie?"

"Yes, Cliff. *We* will return," she told him.

"So consider this a *Cliff*-hanger!" He grinned at Mom, who groaned at his joke.

While we waited for the Shoe Guy to get shoe sizes from Lord Calvert, a familiar-looking boy about my own age came up and said, "Hey, I know you. You're Scott Hansen. I used to go to your school."

I recognized the face but didn't know the name.

He said, "You're McStew's friend. And that other kid—that goofy what's-his-name—is writing a book about you two."

I knew he meant Chip, but I didn't want to say.

"McStew's in California working on a ranch," said the boy.

"Where'd you hear that?" I asked.

"He told me."

"You *saw* him?"

"We were in one of these holes together."

"How long ago was that?" I asked.

"I don't keep a diary. But not that long."

"Did you hear about the fire?"

"That's ancient history."

"Well, did you see him before or after the fire?"

"He said if I made it out west I could work on his ranch. Said he'd even make me foreman," the boy told me.

"Think back. Was it before or after?"

"What's it matter? Look, he didn't burn up in any fire, if that's what's eating you."

"How do you know?"

"Because he's the Gypsy Bandit. He faked his own death."

"Did he say anything about *me*?"

"No, but he had a message for me to give you in case I ever went back to that school. It was—" The boy tried to think.

"It was what?" I felt like shaking him.

"I forget."

"You *forget*?"

"Something really dumb. What I do know is I got plans to go west, just like McStew. Can't you just see me on that ranch?"

"You mean you're running away?"

"Shh! I never said that, so keep your trap shut." He turned to go, then said over his shoulder, "It's me somebody should write a book about." I was about to join the others when the boy called to me from across the room: "I remember what it was now—'Don't forget the green paint.' I *told* you it was something dumb."

I grinned at him and waved. Then before I could change my mind I went over and said to Lord Calvert, "That boy I was just talking to? He said he might run away."

"Who, Barry?" Lord Calvert shook his head. "Poor Barry. He tries that several mornings a week but is always back by lunch. Like the man says, you don't get far on an empty stomach."

The mood in the car was the best it had been all day. Our job was done, we were tired and hungry, and Mr. Stoddard mentioned that his wife would have dinner waiting. He didn't even notice that Lynette sat in the back between me and the Shoe Guy instead of up front with him and Mom.

The Shoe Guy said, "Well, folks, I learned something significant today."

"What's that, Mr. Ragland?" asked Lynette.

"A sense of humor is a terrible thing to waste. I think I'm home at last. Oh, and about this Saturday—" He touched Lynette's father on the shoulder. "In this sad and crazy world there's always room for one more clown. Want to give it a shot?"

Mr. Stoddard pretended he didn't hear.

"You were great back there, Daddy," said Lynette.

"I can teach you magic," the Shoe Guy offered.

"We'll see," said Mr. Stoddard, and the Shoe Guy winked at Lynette.

"Scotty, are you all right?" Lynette asked.

"Fine," I answered, but I was thinking about that boy, that Barry. He'd seen McStew, all right, that was for sure—but was it before or after the fire? That was the question that kept running through my mind. And I kept hearing his words, over and over, not in his own voice, but in McStew's: "Don't forget the green paint."

I felt inside my shirt pocket for the "bullet" that killed Reese, but it was gone. I dug deeper and it just wasn't there. It must've fallen out when everyone was passing me around the room.

"What's the matter?" Lynette smiled. "Did you lose your cuff link again?"

I knew I couldn't ask them to turn around so I could search for some stupid stone. They'd think I was nuts, especially Mr. Stoddard. I slumped down in my seat.

Mom seemed to be in her own world.

"Marie—you okay?" asked the Shoe Guy.

Mom said to Lynette's dad, "Doug, I apologize for what I said earlier. I mean, about not liking you."

"We all say things," said Mr. Stoddard.

"It's just that some people take longer to like than others. I think you're on that list. But deep down you're all right. I mean that."

"Thanks." Mr. Stoddard drove with both hands on the wheel, his eyes straight ahead.

"You did a wonderful thing today. You really came through," Mom said. "Thanks to you, and to the rest of us, those kids will have food in their bellies this Thanksgiving Day."

"Glad to be of service," said Mr. Stoddard, and from where I sat I could see the flicker of a smile.

"That's wonderful to hear," my mother told him, "because guess what? They're going to be hungry again tomorrow."

The smile went away.

"And the next day and the next day and all the days after that," said Mom.

"What are you saying, Marie?" asked the Shoe Guy, leaning forward. "That we should drive around performing good deeds from now on?" I could tell he was ready to swim under ice if she asked him to.

"I'm afraid that's impossible," Mom replied. "However, I do have a plan."

We all held our breaths waiting to hear the plan.

"Because, Cliff, there's something I learned today, too," Mom said. "You don't have to be big in order to make a big difference in someone's life. Look at that Lord Calvert. Those children idolize that man, and all because he's there for them. He's dedicated to putting them on a better road. Well, I've got news for you. All my life I've lived in someone else's shadow—my parents' first, then my husband's, and even my own, never quite knowing what it was I was supposed to do with my days. But now I know. I finally know."

For a minute the only noises came from the car radiator and the snow chains on Mr. Stoddard's tires.

Then Mom said, "I'm going to buy the house next door."

"You're what!" we practically all said at once.

"I'm going to buy the Stewart house. Not by myself, of course. I'll need your help," said Mom. "All of you. No one is likely to move in there, so we'll turn it into a children's home like the ones we saw today. Except we'll find ways of making it even better. Together we can afford it, along with the help of others in the community. Now, who would dare say no? Like the man says, it takes money—and faith. Oh, I can already picture the vegetable garden the kids will plant out back—can't you?"

I don't think anyone was picturing vegetable gardens right then, but the Shoe Guy said, "Marie—a spectacular idea!"

"As for you, Cliff," Mom said, as if seeing it all inside her head, "not just your money, but that gift of yours, making people laugh—can there be anything more valuable? Oh, and Doug? I have plans for you, too."

Mr. Stoddard squeezed the steering wheel.

"I think we'll call it McStew House," said Mom. "My son and I will run it— Did you hear me back there? Did you?"

I could only see the back of her head, but I knew the look on her face, the look she always had when her mind was made up.

"I heard," I said, and turned my face to the window.

"Boy," Lynette leaned close to me, "your mom's really something."

Over to the west, the clouds had finally broken apart and the sun shone through for the first time in days. I imagined it was shining over the place where Wyoming or Utah was, or maybe California. And I whispered to that shiny spot, "Send me a sign—show me you made it."

"What? What did you just say?" asked Lynette.

I turned to see her wonderful smile only an inch from my face, and I said, "She's something, all right—she really is something."

And we rode like that, holding hands.